Dedicated to
Matt

lobe Ja agai

THE CANDLE PEOPLE

GW00711482

by

Jacqueline Puchtler

Grosvenor House
Publishing Limited

This book is published by
Grosvenor House Publishing Ltd
28-30 High Street, Guildford, Surrey, GU1 3EL.
www.grosvenorhousepublishing.co.uk

A CIP record for this book
is available from the British Library

ISBN 978-1-78148-536-1

To Gill, Graham, Simon, Tim and Hazel

Acknowledgements

To Mark for decades of friendship, discussions of life and fiction and professional insights into the human psyche. To Jim for his endless kindnesses, his *hail-fellow-well-met* willingness to help, his inspirational books from various expeditions into the Amazon and for his generosity in proof-reading and Spanish translation. To John for his artistic interpretation of the cover and for the many cups of tea and chats in his gallery. To Simon who has read so much and given me the benefit of his considerable wisdom. To Tim for taking time off from the world of nanotechnology to produce those ingenious candle sketches. To my late friends Usher Rudick who never failed to write, Eleanor Colby who must have been responsible for the sunshine in the Mojave Desert and legendary artist Robert Mercer who, like Cezanne, was painting to the end. To Rob and Sal who renounced their television in order to read. To Debbie for using her significant Information Professional skills to produce the umlaut - and for the laughs! To Sarah, Sally, Rosa, Bill, Pam and Jennie for their encouragement. To dad, a gentleman of the old school, who, despite having passed away is ever-present - and to my amazing mum who writes and is an inspiration in all that she does.

Chapter 1

It's true that Catherine was not a prisoner in her own home. The doors were not locked, the windows were not bolted. Yet she felt incarcerated, like the Lady of Shalott, condemned in her captive tower to view the world through a looking-glass, a world of shadows in which she could not fully participate for she had no idea where they cast her and in whose image. Truth was ill-determined by mirrors, which reflected only details, apparent yet hollow; emerald eyes, ebony hair, cardinal lips. They offered no recognition of identity beyond the superficial, no insights into the endless kaleidoscope of half-remembered names and faces that spun around inside her head, amongst them her own. She was like a featureless map, a story without words, left to drift into the unknown, to weave tales of better worlds, worlds of faraway Camelots and red-cross knights.

She opened the door of the old farmhouse as if to reassure herself of her liberty and shivered, chilled by the harsh gusts of a wind that whistled plaintively through the pine trees beyond like a high-pitched elegy. It was fear that kept her shackled to this house, she knew that. Yet somewhere out there beyond this remote and inhospitable place was the key to her existence. It began to rain lightly and it was then that she noticed the rainbow, its colours as sharply defined as in a naïve painting. She half turned to close the door when a key fell from above as if from the golden part of the rainbow arc. She stooped to retrieve it, happy to accept miracles. Its serrated edge dispersed small amounts of sunlight amongst the bladed grass, turning them from olivine to viridian, the tiny ladybird nearby from crimson to scarlet. The ladybird lifted minute wings and landed on the key which had a thread of cotton attached to it. She wondered what or who she was meant to unlock with it. Herself perhaps? It was then that she noticed the two magpies on the distant fencing and smiled. Damn, an end to miracles. Someone was probably going crazy at that precise moment looking for it. 'Show me the light,' she thought to herself, 'Aurora Borealis or Aurora Australis, I'm indifferent to direction. Just show me the light before the world turns monochrome in his memory.'

He was the greatest mystery of all, the personification of her worst fears and she could imagine no solitude that would have driven her into his arms, no fear for which he could have offered consolation. She had often tried to recapture the sentiments that she knew must once have been there before he became just an unhappy thought, when his existence for her was more than transcendental, when he was a person rather than just a persona - *persona non grata*, but her memory denied her even that small benevolence. It was a marriage of inconvenience. Perhaps in the tradition of holiday romances, too much sun had affected her judgement, or too many beaches liberally sprinkled with hardened, sun-tanned bodies. She must have drunk too many margaritas at the old cantina to know what she was doing. Lost in Margaritaville. So much tequila that she forgot herself, woke up realising what she'd done - she'd eaten the worm from the bottle, joined herself in perfect harmony like "Ebony and Ivory." It was surely doomed from the first.

What a curious journal her life would make if only she possessed the ability to document it. She hoped that one day she would. She felt as though she was on a great quest, an embarkation for home perhaps, after years at sea. And what a huge relief it would be to find something as tractable as dry land beneath her feet, and, after tons of ballast weighing heavily on each conscious hour, to have nothing more to carry than a knowledge of who she was.

All she really knew was that she had awoken four years ago, was brought back to consciousness by the pains of labour with no recollection of anything prior to that moment other than a knowledge of this farmhouse. Confused and afraid she'd grappled to scale the walls of her contractions while trying to remember something of what had happened to her. But it was all blackouts and invasion, like Armageddon, her own bellicose belly in front of her, sheets a bloodied battlefield. And then the baby slipped from her and she heard it cry. At least she had thought she did. Later she realised the sound was her own, muffled and internal. Despite her confusion she felt an immediate and intense love for her daughter as she held her in her arms, her carmine lips slightly parted, her eyes closed like dermal shells. She struggled to remember the time when she had been conceived or when she had simply been a small punctuation mark, lost somewhere in the expanse of her womb, but she could not. All she knew was that they were beginning life together; the world was a mystery to them both. The nurses must have understood this. Afterwards they bathed her as if she had been a helpless newborn too. She remembered the initial feeling of physical discomfort as her toes had touched the water, and the odd feeling of being naked in front of strangers and not caring, the sensation of having compassion swept through her hair in the guise of shampoo and of the queer arrangement of the soap suds, laced with the blood in which she sat and which belonged to her.

Her mind returned to the domesticity of her present life and she switched on the oven. The food she had prepared earlier would take several hours to cook, long enough to perform the list of duties she had set herself, though many of them were to be conducted outside and it had begun to rain. Instead she decided to switch on the newly purchased television, an acquisition *he* might have hoped, would stave off this new restlessness in her which would have frightened him more than the violence of his feelings for her. The television set was unlike that of her friends in the cottages by the cliffs which boasted the latest plasma screen and was slender enough for a wall hanging. Bought at the local auction its proportions were bulky and graceless and it awoke slowly from its periods of dormancy, sound followed languorously by vision.

A blonde, middle-aged woman appeared on the screen, whose soft voice and reassuring manner saved the exposure of her ample bosom in its low-cut blouse, from vulgarity. She turned to her male co-host. 'What an exciting line up we have today.'

'Absolutely,' he smiled showing discomfortingly white teeth, 'winning recipes, your chance to win £1,000, the latest film news… but first of course, and of particular interest to any art lovers out there… now we're all used to the type of controversy caused by the art world - the Turner Prize for example, every year artists extending the boundaries of what we think of as real art, Damien Hirst's cows in formaldehyde or Tracy Emin's *Untidy Bed*, but I don't think that we've ever had any contemporary artist claiming to be the reincarnation of another artist before. So without further ado,' he turned to his guest, 'we welcome John Smith. Not,' he smiled lavishly, 'the most promising name for someone who claims such provenance.'

'No, I agree,' the man smiled indulgently, 'it's a great name for church or ceremonial purposes but if you were to shout it at the station I expect half the men on the platform would answer.'

Catherine watched transfixed. There was a familiarity about this man that she couldn't quite place, like a town that you knew you'd passed through but couldn't locate on the map.

'But do you really believe Mr Smith,' the woman enquired incredulously, 'that you are the reincarnation of Francisco de Goya, arguably the greatest artist of all time. I mean, it seems highly improbable that… do you not think perhaps, that the artist you speak of, with whom you claim such apparent, um, *affiliation*, for want of a better word, may simply have influenced your work to such an extent that these delusions…'

'Delusions?' The artist gazed pointedly into the depths of her ceaseless cleavage. 'I don't do delusions.'

'Perhaps *delusions* is the wrong word. Do you think Dick?' She looked for support from her co-host who had noted with some irritation John Smith's interest in his partner.

'Yes, you're right Trudi, though I do see what you mean.' He turned acidly to their guest. 'What Trudi means I think, is that perhaps you find some comfort in the belief that you are this great artist reincarnated. After all, it would absolve the need for originality wouldn't it?'

'Originality! Who could prefer originality to a talent like Goya's? Do you know anyone else who can paint like me?'

'You have an undeniable talent certainly but that doesn't mean... Goya was born in the eighteenth century at a time...'

'Yes time...'

Catherine, felt there was a great deal of artifice in John Smith's face which otherwise lacked complication. It was a good face, handsome, a strong, intelligent face that denied any possibility of madness.

'Sometimes,' John Smith reclined into billowing cushions, 'sometimes time seems to race backward like a Bavarian clock so that the past seems more real than the present. It's like being burdened with two lives - as if one isn't enough.'

The pretty hostess leaned forward revealing yet more of her copious breasts. Her questioning, which had begun hesitantly, seemed to have gathered momentum. 'But the artist whose identity you claim Mr Smith, or may I call you John...?'

'With breasts like that you can call me anything you like.'

'Well really...' Her co-host seemed lost for words.

Catherine smiled broadly so that rivulets of the water she was drinking spilled from her generous mouth.

The hostess regained her composure. 'As I was saying, the artist whose identity you claim, was born into turbulent political times and I would have thought that his art cannot be separated from the wider historical picture. I mean, his renowned struggle with his own allegiances caused him great emotional suffering. How do you attribute the fact that, forgive me, er, John, you do not appear to be suffering, either from the physical disabilities of deafness and impaired motor activity that plagued him or from the emotional burden that accompanies inner despair.'

John Smith raised his brows in apparent indignation. 'Suffering... what do you know of my suffering?'

'Of course we're not art historians,' Trudi was unremitting, 'but I personally see very few similarities between you and Goya.'

'Yes,' Dick recovered his voice, 'I believe it was Huelsenbeck who said, I quote,' he checked his notes, 'that "artists are creatures of their epoch and that the highest art will be that in which its conscious content presents the thousand-fold problems of the day, the art which has been shattered by the explosions of last week, which is forever trying to collect its limbs after yesterdays crash."' He looked pleased with himself. 'These are not such times Mr. Smith, at least from your own perspective and you don't appear to be devoid of any limbs, metaphorically or otherwise.'

'Perhaps you just haven't learned to look. As Matisse once said, and now *I* quote, though less elaborately, "seeing is in itself an art." And suffering comes in many guises. It would be remarkably insular to assume that the monopoly for sadness belongs only to those found hanging in their basements. War, rape, torture, famine - these are not the only sufferings. Death is easy. It's love that proves the biggest torment for an artist.' Catherine felt herself nodding absently. 'But then I wouldn't expect you to understand that. How could you? Other people's emotions only have significance if we can identify them in ourselves. Life seems pointless now, but it goes on all the same, impelled by an inner necessity.' He paused. 'I can't say that sleep comes easily without her, but it finds a way.'

'Of course, your infamous love affair with the Duchess of Alba...' The hostess raised a sympathetic eyebrow. 'Can you tell us about that? Did you really have a physical relationship? The point is still hotly debated. In fact Dick, wasn't there a film made about it?'

'Yes, by Carlos Saura I believe.' Dick's eyes narrowed with intensity. 'But what has really outraged, or let's say stunned, the art world, is that, not only do you claim you had an *affair* with the Duchess of Alba, but also that you had an illegitimate child together - a daughter. And furthermore you claim that you painted the Duchess of Alba with your child and that, to avoid scandal the painting was smuggled out of the country and ended up, of all places, in South West England.' He paused briefly for laughter. 'Along the way you claim, many were tortured by the Spanish Inquisition for assisting you and one young girl was executed for hiding the painting briefly in her room. I mean...' his expression indicated amusement, 'these claims are incredible and completely unsubstantiated. Were it not for the fact that you do, indeed have an extraordinary talent for painting like the great master, I doubt that anyone would have given you the time of day. I mean, can you give us any reasons why we should believe such an incredible tale?'

Catherine watched with interest John Smith's expression which wavered between amusement and irritation. 'I know what you want. You want me to spill the beans, human beans, has-beens, all mingled up. Well I can't. I don't know what to say and fear, yes fear, that whatever I say will be maligned or deliberately misunderstood.' He laughed then as if a spell had been broken. 'Ahhhhh, memories, sweet memories - "cigarettes and whisky and wild, wild women." It's funny but somehow I think that if I tell you all, you'll probably end up feeling that you just can't help me, that you need help yourself.'

'Are you saying that you are still troubled by the affair? One would imagine that after two hundred years even the most resolute of broken hearts would mend. But then,' the host smiled loftily, 'she *was* very beautiful.'

John Smith seemed lost in reveries of past worlds. 'Sometimes her image is so vivid. I can remember the way she laughed and danced and painted rainbows. Trouble was in the air even then, but at the time we didn't realise that there was no turning back, only that the torment of existence could so easily be forgotten. But I think I've said enough. If I let myself slip back, think how much we meant to each other... well, once you do that you're as good as lost.'

'No, no, please go on. It's fascinating, isn't it Dick?'

'Absolutely. In fact, I don't think we've ever met anyone quite like you, have we Trudi?'

'No, never.'

'You must come back. Will you do that?'

'I've not gone yet.'

'No, no, of course, do carry on. You were saying.'

'Well,' John Smith eased himself further into the burgundy, leather sofa, 'we met at a time I suppose when we both wanted to end the horror of isolation, me as an artist, her as a woman flagrantly misunderstood. Despite our differing backgrounds we knew we were meant for each other so there was no need for games or social conventions. She led me to a room. The room was hot and stuffy and dark I remember, so very dark, risen heat hung in the atmosphere ready to bake your head. That's probably why we spent so much time horizontal on her sofa, you might call it a couch - like this one. Anyway,' he paused, 'there's nothing really of interest to hear unless you're one of the characters in the story book of course.' He glanced leisurely at Trudi. 'Fancy popping between the sheets with me do you?' His eyes levelled at Dick. 'Or do you simply want to look at the pictures - choose a nice picky to meep over?'

'I can't help but notice a certain hostility.' Dick's steely composure was uncharacteristically shaken. 'But we're simply trying to lighten the load John. That's the whole point of this interview. It's not an interrogation.'

John Smith laughed a hollow laugh. 'That's what she used to do, lighten the load, sometimes with her mouth and sometimes, sometimes...'

'Please go on.' Dick's face was suddenly animated.

'But please keep in mind,' Trudi added professionally, 'that this is daytime TV.'

John Smith smiled lazily. 'All I can remember right now are her long, dark tresses floating in endless summer days that will never again see the grim light of reality.'

'Okay well,' the hostess paused, disappointed, 'if you don't want to talk about her then talk about yourself. Let me see now. Goya was born in Aragon wasn't he?'

'Yes,' Dick interjected, 'what is your earliest recollection of life, of being?'

John Smith paused for a moment, then smiled the smile of a man who knew he had been dealt a winning hand and saw no advantage in disguising it. 'Yes okay, I see it, my mother being wheeled into the labour room. I was still inside her at the time you see. She was a big woman, paps full, already dilated in the eyes and between the thighs. I felt her hands resting above me as my body swayed in the gushing current provoked only hours before by the amplified banging of my father's brutal rutting as he nudged her womb.' His words had agitated the colour of the hostess's pale skin for which he seemed pleased.

'You have an excellent memory Mr. Smith.'

'Thank you.'

Dick, half listening to the producer while glancing cursorily at his notes, said sternly, 'We're just getting a message to say you must tone down your language. As Trudi's already said we're not anywhere near the 9 o'clock watershed.'

'Dreary me.'

'An intriguing portrayal of your father though.'

'He sounds like a rather insensitive man,' Trudi added perceptively.

'Truth is I don't remember much about him. I remember him chiding me for the usual stuff, you know,' he studied her as if for signs of gullibility, 'splashing in deep puddles, playing too loud on my bassoon.'

Dick's usually slick and oleaginous manner was broken momentarily by the hooting of his own belly laughter. 'I must say I'm finding it very hard to take you seriously. But then with Goya *madness* of course was also an issue. Or should I say more pertinently, "the sleep of reason." Has it produced any monsters yet John?' Smugness broke into his attractive features.

John Smith smiled an elusive smile. 'As someone once said, "It's not madness that we should fear but the suffocating limitations of sanity." I don't have a problem with madness.'

'Er,' the hostess smiled a gentle, placatory smile, 'perhaps now would be a good time to look at some of your artwork John. For example, the portrait you did recently - it is of course the woman who obsesses you is it not, though her face seems rather more angular than in the more familiar versions of the Black and the White Duchess.'

Behind them a canvas was unveiled.

Catherine's glass loosened in her dank palm. Gazing from within the canvas a woman smiled at her, a languid, knowing smile that curved alizarin lips and across which fell luxurious, thick, black hair. There was an exquisite frailty to her paleness amidst so much that was dark - the darkness of her hair, the dark wretchedness of the studio in which she had been painted. Oddly it was at that point that Catherine noticed John Smith's hand which was placed languidly upon his thigh. It seemed disproportionately large, like the hand of Michelangelo's David. John Smith too she felt, was exposed as a flawed masterpiece, his hand strangely at odds with his supple frame and the chiselled beauty of his face. The woman in the painting seemed not to notice the sombre darkness of the world around her. But for how long would that remain? How long would she have remained insensitive to the dark, dingy studio, to the troubled, dark eyes of the artist that looked upon her now, eyes which had seen the horrors of the world in myriad forms? Catherine felt her nerves quiver. Her own image stared directly at her from within the darkness of the canvas. This was she, as true an effigy as any photograph and she reeled from its starkness as if stricken by the coarse, collusive hand that had created her.

Chapter 2

It was strange, Catherine thought, how sleep sometimes devoured you while at other times it spat you out. These days sleep came to her, or she to it, reluctantly, more out of necessity, though there was a strong desire not to sleep at all, since by sleeping, not only did you miss half of your life, but for all you knew, it could be the better half. Though her eyes were closed she could feel his presence, see the look of hate that, unlike the mercurial nature of facial expression, remained fixed, as if worn into a rock after centuries of tidal beatings. How, she wondered, did this face perceive their union? It had certainly paid its price for loving her. And she, the maid of the sea as he once called her, had played her part in its immutable quality, had anchored it in its joylessness. They had barely communicated other than in irritation, yet she knew that he would never willingly have given her up. Like a tobacco habit he had become addicted to this joyless life with her and the child he had never acknowledged. Her thoughts turned to John Smith's portrait. Had it really resembled her so precisely or had she imagined it? Was her desire for a past so strong that she had unwittingly altered the features on the canvas in order to acquire one? Perhaps it was now *she* blowing smoke rings, seeing visions.

As sleep denied her she decided to write in her diary which she kept hidden downstairs under the floorboards and which she had neglected of late. She sat in the parlour in her dressing gown oblivious to the cool night air. Oddly the diary gave her a sense of freedom. In this sense writing had an unassailable advantage over other forms of communication. It was possible to use your pen to forgive yourself anything, to go anywhere, to write yourself a new world if you wished, the only pressure being in the anticipation of what you might write. She took up her pen and began.

"Yes, I still want to go to distant places and see wondrous things. Yes I still have dreams. I do occasionally suffer bouts of self doubt and depression. There are a number of fine lines on my face and no, I am not handling the tumble toward mid-life with dignity. I have a violent urge to have a tattoo etched onto an anatomically stimulating area of my body and an even greater urge to display it in public. Forgive me, I am trying to contain myself and be somewhat mature in my writing but it's too demanding."

The clock struck another fruitless hour on the mantelshelf, the place where most families displayed photographs of their happiest times. But she had lived long enough, even in her renaissance to know that smiling faces did not always denote happiness. There was something fraudulent, she thought, about a photographic representation of events, thoughts being effectively concealed behind the deceitful tradition of smiling for cameras. One learnt nothing about oneself from them; they were designed to obscure not enlighten, especially those at Christmas, the loneliest time of the year, a time of enforced merriment when crackers were pulled and everyone wore paper crowns like comic royalty. But if you looked closer at the snaps, behind the eyes or in an unguarded moment, there were vague glimmers of sadness or disapproval. She continued writing.

"Yes, I want to escape my life, or rediscover it, to have a chance to be me again, to feel the wind in my face and excitement in my breath. No more pretending - the love has gone, if it ever existed. No more copulating in desperation searching for the tenderness that is no longer there. An end to moribund marriages. The Decree Absolute will slip with quiet dignity through the fringed letterbox. The final penetration. There will be no sound as it falls onto the linoleum. No echo from the clashing of temperaments or the machine gun firing of solicitor's letters. The air will hold in its stillness a suggestion of a truce." She thought again of the painting. *"Today I saw myself and want to know where I came from. I hope it's from somewhere exotic, remote - somewhere where it is still possible to breathe unpolluted air and meet unpolluted people. Perhaps I will rediscover myself there and retire in this new-found paradise, Panama perhaps - untouched by greedy, despoiling 'civilization,' with beautiful rainforests, proud Indians, overgrown remnants of the Spanish Conquistadors, clear blue waters, gorgeous reefs sporting a thousand colourful fish. I will open a small hotel perhaps and never lose myself again. What shall I call it? The Last Stop Motel, I believe."*

She smiled at the indulgence of her written words. Then she heard his voice drowning her thoughts and her anxiety returned. 'Catherine, come to bed Catherine.' She shut the diary abruptly and pushed it down the side of the sofa, still partially distracted by thoughts of her own Arcadia. It would be hot and humid and there would be bugs and a general air of jungle madness, but lots of gin. She said out loud, 'Play it again Sam,' then stiffened as she felt his presence, irritated, as though her words were a bitter response to his request.

'Come to bed,' she heard repeated. 'You'll be tired in the morning.'

She replied inwardly, 'I'll be up in a minute.' Without seeing she recognised his suspicious glance.

'You were gone a long time today. Where did you go? What took you so long?'

'I really don't remember.'

Alone again, his image disabled, she sought out her diary in order to complete the final page. Glancing again at the mantelpiece she wrote,

"So sing Magpies, Jackdaws, Jays and Rooks alike. Sing you family of Crows. Kraa, kraa, prook, prook. The ravens are leaving the tower. It's the end of an era of kings and queens."

In the morning when she awoke she was alone. It was still early and she began to doze when her daughter Emily climbed wearily into bed beside her. She said, 'I don't want to go to school today,' and drifted back to sleep, resolute face barely visible beneath the substantial layer of duvet. It was at times like these, Catherine thought, that one had to confront the vexed and punishing question as to why one bothered to have children at all. She lay digesting Emily's words, troubled despite her conviction that there was a degree of guile behind them. Emily could sense her concern and reinforced it at every opportunity. Not entirely without reason. Her teacher was fond of punishment it seemed, not the knuckle-rapping kind but the more sinister, punitive measures - the ridicule that prompted classroom sniggering, the weariness in a voice that had to explain twice, the weighty threat of the invisible yet ubiquitous dunce's cap. Emily was a quiet girl. Her teacher, Catherine knew, would perceive her quietness as a lack of understanding and school would become a constant battleground for her, not to prove her intelligence but to avoid the inevitable punishment that came with not caring to.

Every morning Emily's uniform became curiously misplaced, her limbs ached, her appetite faltered. Breakfast was a scene of gloomy belligerence, cereal stirred defiantly then left to congeal, monosyllabic responses supplemented occasionally with emotive outbursts counteracted by Catherine's reasoned responses. They would leave the house late, drained and unsated, neither of them happy. Catherine wondered whether another visit to the school would produce anything other than hostility. She thought of the stern, impatient face of Emily's teacher, how the vertical lines between the brows deepened and the horizontal ones crossing over them had likened her forehead to a game of noughts and crosses. She had felt like putting a large X in the middle square. The middle square, it had always been stipulated, was the most strategic of starts. These thoughts occupied her till, just as she was beginning to drift into sleep, the alarm clock repeated the process of disturbance.

External noise shifted Emily's composure, the small mouth tightened and the eyes motioned beneath their lids. 'I don't want to go to school today,' she repeated, 'I don't feel well enough.'

'Don't worry,' Catherine heard herself saying, 'you're not going today.' She felt Emily's tightened form relax, the effects on herself being equally pacific.

CHAPTER 3

Some distance north east John Smith dozed in a railway carriage, travelling home after a late evening meeting with his agent in London. He was in the middle of a strange dream when voices startled him into a flickering awareness of the new day. He felt cold and disorientated in the carriage seat. His limbs ached and his mouth was dry. 'Bones and buggers and curses Moriarty.' He sat up stiffly, tired, but disinclined to recline, loath to slide back into the arms of Morpheus lest he was kept there, subsumed by unconscious fears and yearnings. The rude awakening had not entirely erased details of his dream, central to which had been the painting in which his Duchess featured. They had danced, he and Alba, together amidst the trembling, impasto-layered darkness. What had he said in the interview? "Laughed and danced and painted rainbows?" The sinuous lines of her thighs had tightened as she'd moved in time with his. Strange that he should remember this. The residual power of her image curved his mouth into a reluctant half-smile as a chink in the carriage blinds threw a crude light into the shabby uncertainty of his surroundings.

The carriage in which he sat was tired looking, defaced by age and graffiti and he felt a certain comfort in that since it meant he owed it no reverence. Usually he loved travelling by train. He always made a point of arriving at the station as early as he could and would stand for the longest time on the platform observing the confluence of massive, intractable metal bodies of trains plunging in and out of the station, punctuated by the sounds of whistles and announcements of arrivals and departures. People of every specification would emerge from their attendant carriages onto hostile platforms grey with age and utility and he would trace their steps with his intense artist's eye, endeavouring for a transient moment to penetrate the surface of some nameless person whose expression or gait may momentarily have captured his imagination. Rail was the most compelling mode of transport for an artist. The lulling, intoxicating rhythm of the train, coupled with the proximity of strangers created an illusion of intimacy that he found less demanding than the genuine article.

But today he noticed no one and the tremulous motion, coupled with the nicotine-stained air evoked only nausea. The washing in the small, terraced gardens signalled them past the outer suburbs into the countryside; he could no longer blame the city since even the bordering meadows, distorted by his mood, appeared to rise and fall at severer angles. The only incongruity was the sky that held in its paltering blueness the most vibrant spectrum of colours. John Smith glanced at the rainbow that was emerging outside. "Laughed and danced and painted rainbows." Everything reminded him of her. The cheerfulness of it was onerous. He would have liked to have reached up and dislodged it. Goya had become his own private nightmare. As a man with a low boredom threshold he was now tired of this game. It had been his agent's idea as a strategy to raise his artistic profile but he could not have predicted how his claim would escalate. The television broadcast had been the final humiliation. He now found himself a subject in his own *Caprichos*, fantasy series, one of the bats in the belfry perhaps, a statement of self-imposed schizophrenia. And worst of all he was caught up in a love affair with a woman who had been pushing up daisies for the last two centuries and who, oddly enough, had begun to obsess his waking hours. She was so like Maria that the two had become almost inseparable in his psyche. It was the only part of the whole charade that seemed paradoxically, more real than reality. Were the situation not so ridiculous it might have been amusing. 'Idiot,' he muttered, louder than intended. 'You idiot.'

'Come again?' A tattooed man sitting opposite looked menacingly in his direction.

Oh, he thought, ignoring the stare, to come again in the grip of her tender thighs that clung like wild rose to his ill-used and embittered flesh. But she was gone, irretrievably gone, his own Alba, drowned, the last sighting of her disappearing beneath the water, beyond his reach. This vision still haunted his waking moments. He looked aimlessly out of the carriage window. That sweet smell, was it her? He half expected her image to materialise in the landscape in some foliate guise. His agent, conversely, found his obsession hilarious.

'Don't get me wrong. It's not hard to understand. You lost the love of your life and it's very sad so now you paint her as the Duchess of Alba. But look, not that I'm averse to the older woman but two hundred years is a little extreme don't you think?'

'That's right you laugh, but I just can't seem to get her out of my head. When I paint it's like she's there in the room guiding my hand.'

'You sure it's when you're painting?'

'Very amusing.'

'Well just remember that we made this whole thing up. It's not a self-fulfilling prophesy. You've just done too much research that's all. Like a method actor you're living the part. But don't get like...you know, who was it that said that his inner life had become more important to the point where he now travelled in his mind and lived in it to a large extent?'

'Well it wasn't Mr Bean. He never says anything.'

His agent laughed. 'That's right, see the funny side. Anyway, find yourself a real woman. They should be falling over themselves now you've had all this publicity.'

'Yeah right, Christ,' he gestured to his face, 'I suddenly feel old. And there are a number of things growing from my eyelids. Can you see them? The sort of growths that old people get. I expect Goya had them too. It's the stress of keeping up appearances. It's completely out of hand. I mean, did you watch the interview? "What's your earliest recollection of life Mr Smith." Give me a break!'

'That's exactly what it is - a break, a little gift.' His agent smiled. 'Your work has never been in such demand. And you've never made so much money. Nor have I come to that! What does it matter what people think? People are having conversations about art because of you. People love the controversy art creates. Think of the Turner Prize. That's what it's all about. You've got exhibitions, the interview for Art International, the commissions. Who cares whether you're a phoney?'

'Well I just might - if not out of moral indignation then maybe because of the energy it's costing me trying to remember all the lies I've told.'

His agent laughed. 'You'll thank me one day when your paintings are selling for the same prices as Vettriano's.'

'That kitsch crap.'

'Hey don't knock it. The guy's laughing all the way to the bank. Anyway,' he added provocatively, 'for someone who says he's uncomfortable with dishonesty, you seem to have embraced your role quite well. I mean, I know this whole thing was my idea but the part in your interview about the lost Goya painting of Alba and her child that Goya apparently fathered was an unnecessary embellishment wouldn't you say? Delightful, but surplus to requirements.'

John Smith looked sheepish. 'It wasn't an embellishment it was the truth in a manner of speaking.'

'Now I am getting worried about you.'

'No, I mean, well, I painted a portrait of Maria with our unborn child in anticipation of the event. She was heavily pregnant at the time of the accident and I lost them both.'

'I'm sorry, I didn't know about the child.'

'It was one of the most accomplished paintings I've ever managed. I don't know, maybe it was cathartic as I seem to remember having some premonition that something would happen, but I was driven to finish it like never before. For weeks I barely slept until it was completed. Then it disappeared. You remember when I first employed you, I told you about the theft at my studio?'

'Vaguely, but you didn't tell me about the nature of the painting.'

'No, well, it didn't seem appropriate at the time. Losing Maria was the worst thing that ever happened to me. The painting was another great loss. I'd immortalised her in oil, not just her, but our child, the child of my imagination, and now even that was taken away. It wasn't something that I felt like talking about at the time.' He paused. 'You know, when someone very dear to you first dies you can conjure them up in an instant, their face, the taste and smell of them. You dread the inevitable day when you struggle to manage that. The painting helped. Of course I have photographs, but it's not the same as a painting. Paintings have soul. The mention of Goya's love child in the interview, well,' his eyes lowered with the gravity of feeling, 'it may have been a lie but it was the only part of the interview that seemed real to me. Admittedly I got a bit carried away with the Spanish Inquisition.'

'Hey, never let truth stand in the way of a good story.'

The train sped forth and the tattooed man aggravated him simply by breathing. Although it was not Christmas he felt the acrimonious character of Scrooge stir from within. Maybe he should go into town later and shoot out all the lights with that old BB gun he had acquired in his wasted youth some days ago. Let's face it, he flicked cigarette ash absently into the atmosphere, defying new regulations, there was no Santa Claus, there was no such thing as a free lunch and no one cared if we lived or died except ourselves, so baaaah humbug, take that you tattooed moron. Soon he would need to return to London for the opening of his exhibition for which he needed to summon every ounce of cordiality. A speech was no doubt expected, some interaction with the audience. The gentle chug of the carriage lulled him into disgruntled repose as the landscape changed yet again into cityscape and Cambridge drew him into its inveterate and seductive presence. Above the sky seemed unchanging and his last conscious thought before arrival was of the rainbow - a reluctant, nostalgic consciousness of its presence and that of the illusive pot of gold that was supposedly concealed beneath.

CHAPTER 4

Catherine whistled like a kettle on a hob, a tunelessness generated by nervous anticipation. Having been confined to the house for several weeks she could hardly suppress her elation at having liberated herself from its suffocating presence yet she did so with fear and trepidation. She glanced back at its gloomy, silent frame, shadows cast about it like some eerie Gothic setting and wished she need never return, yet still she struggled to walk away. She deliberately took a convoluted route as it meant they were unlikely to be observed from the roadside. She felt him watching, sensed his dislike of her forging any life outside his own companionship. She sensed in him too a deep, internalised aggression the intensity of which was revealed only through a deafening and impermeable silence.

Beyond the nearby thicket of trees was a bridle path which led after a mile or so to a row of thatched cottages lining the crude pavement beside the moist, dirt track, their tiny windows thickly muddied from passing traffic. Beyond these cottages was a post office and a pub called The Wayfarer, and further still a small grocery store. Thereafter the path steepened dramatically until the sea was mistily visible.

'Look Emily,' Catherine lifted the small child above her shoulders, 'the sea.'

'Can we go in it?'

'Yes, when it's warmer. But not right now or you'll catch a cold.'

'I love it here. Can we go to see Rosy and Anja every day?'

'You know we can't. You have to go to school sometimes.'

The small girl skipped ahead happily, her short legs sturdy in their red sandals, embracing the damp air as spontaneously as the noisy gulls that traversed the coast line. After some time Emily veered off the beaten track and, observing a rabbit, followed it into a wooded area nearby.

'Emily, come back.' Catherine followed her daughter into the darkness of the wood. Emily had disappeared out of sight now and though Catherine knew she could not have gone far, she felt a panic rise in her. 'Emily, where are you?' she shouted.

'Over here.'

Catherine followed her daughter's faint voice through the thicket of trees. Emily had stopped in her tracks and was pointing upward. 'Look a church.'

She was right. Ahead of them a spire protruded through a cluster of oak and lime trees which now and again, between leafy attire afforded glimpses of the church nave. They walked toward it. The larger trees thinned out after a while leaving mainly yews and hedgerow. Catherine stared up at the massive tower. On the gable end of the north porch a fairly new cross had been erected which looked slightly incongruous against the ageing timber. She felt with a certainty that she had been there before but she couldn't remember exactly when or in what capacity.

'I want to see inside it.'

Catherine too was curious. She checked her watch. 'Another time Emily. We have to hurry now.'

'Do you promise?'

'Yes, now come on. We have to go.'

Retracing their steps Catherine rediscovered the path and after some time they arrived outside a row of five large, terraced cottages about half a mile from the knurled coast line. Her friend Anja owned the middle one with the bottle green, peeling doorway, which was flanked by cottages of comparable decay, one of which was owned by Rosy. Anja and Rosy were her only friends and she felt that life would have been insufferable without them. A large woman appeared on the doorstep. She was wearing brightly coloured clothes that augmented the red in her hair and which suited her vivacity which was evident even from a distance. She made her way forward, loping easily on her formidable calves and eventually clasping Catherine in her animated bosom. Anja was an artist who painted bold, expressionistic canvasses which covered every wall of the cottage. Just lately she seemed to be experimenting with the surrealist style, strange, dream-logic creations with absurd juxtapositions.

'Catherine, I've been dying to see you. We were so worried Rosy and I that we think of coming to see you despite your dislike of visitors.' Catherine found her presence and the accent, still thick and laden with endearing grammatical errors, reassuring. 'We talk about it and then, guess what, guess what? No you will NEVER guess, not in a million years. We watch this programme on the television and suddenly you are there! Tis unbelievable. And Rosy, she is here too. She will tell you. She is pulling what you English call a *sicky*. She says she feels unwell but I know it is just so that she can sit with me and gossip about her latest affair with one of those little boys she likes. This latest is only twenty-two and such a skinny little thing. I tell her she should go for someone her own age but it is not for me to say. Come, come.' Catherine felt her excitement rise and combine with intense relief.

Inside the cottage she noted the wallpaper, jaundiced with age, and the curtains, which were bright orange throughout and which didn't meet in the middle. Fortunately overgrown shrubs outside made Anja invulnerable to the inquisitive but the room was always dark as a consequence. The walls were covered in Anja's artwork, bright and strident and endearingly familiar. Catherine always remembered the room with great affection. The cottage was deceptively large with an extension at the back that incorporated Anja's studio and a downstairs bedroom.

Their chatter was interrupted by Hilda, Anja's mother-in-law who appeared, stooped in the tradition of the very old, bearing her crutch like a trident. The crutch helped support the old woman's movements as she wavered on her prosthetic leg. Her tiny eyes were enveloped for the most part by loose flesh furrowed deeply between the brows. It was a face, Catherine thought, like an old world map, where features of reference could only be vaguely determined between the deep lines of longitude and latitude. Most compelling of all were the whiskers on her chin that were as long and severe as a cat's. She settled into one of the armchairs.

'*Na Ja,* I'm just going to make tea for my friends Hilda. Would you like tea and a sandwich maybe?'

'What kind of sandwich?'

'Whatever you like.'

'Anything will do.'

'Okay, cheese then.'

'No, no anything but cheese.'

'Okay, I will get you ham and pickle.'

'No, no I've gone off pickle.'

'Tuna then or salmon spread?'

'No, no. I'll have marmite. But just a thin scraping mind.'

Anja and Catherine withdrew to the kitchen.

'It is like having another child.' Anja took the marmite out of the cupboard. 'Oh, the marmite is out-of-date.'

Catherine smiled. 'I don't think it will make much difference at her age.'

There was a sudden flurry of activity as several small children clambered excitedly down the stairs shouting Emily's name. 'Bruno, Hanz, Ilse, Lucy, you do not appear so sick now you see Emily. You are very naughty children all of you. You will be punished very harshly if you don't go outside this very minute.' Anja shouted something in German but the children, seemingly immune to the severity of her threats, continued to spring like jumping jacks around Catherine. Anja began to chase them around the kitchen, while they squealed excitedly like piglets. With her long, lank hair loosely plaited and her large bosom locked inside a bodice dress that emphasised the thickness of her waist, Anja looked something like a pantomime dame. She suddenly changed tactics. 'Outside now and you will all have cake later.' She had long since reached the conclusion that bribery was a necessary part of child rearing, and she no longer chastised herself for partaking in it.

'Here, I'll make the sandwich.' Catherine finished the sandwich and took it to the old lady who took a bite from it.

'Did I say not too much marmite?'

'You did.'

After a moment she put her plate down. 'Well, I've done the best I can with it but there was too much marmite on it.'

'Don't worry,' Catherine said good-humouredly. 'I'll give the rest to the birds, it'll put feathers on their chests.'

'I used to give Twinkletoes a bit when he was alive.'

'Her budgerigar,' Anja explained. 'She talks about him all the time.'

'Oh, I see.' She watched Hilda's whiskers twitch with emotion. 'You should get another one.'

'It wouldn't be the same.'

'What colour was he?'

'Green.'

'Ah, lots of green budgerigars around.'

'Twinkletoes was more than just green.'

The idle profundity of the old woman's remark added pathos to the sadness of her expression. Just then the door to the sitting room opened and Rosy appeared, a striking woman in her late thirties, rather too thin, with a wide smile full of predatory, white teeth set in fleshy, pink gums. 'Well, well,' she kissed Catherine on the cheek, 'if it isn't the Duchess of Alba herself. Should we curtsey?' She laughed uproariously.

Catherine's relief intensified. 'You saw the interview then. It wasn't just my imagination. The painting really resembled me?'

'Resembled? Are you kidding? It was your mirror image. We suspected you must have been posing for this guy on the quiet. Hey, we should call a newspaper. I can just see the headlines. "*Duchess Returns from the Dead.*" You might make a small fortune, which of course you would want to share with your only friends. I couldn't believe it. All that time Anja wasted at art school studying the crude eroticism of the German Expressionists and other twentieth century art movements when all the time we had the mistress of the great Francisco de Goya in our midst.'

Tears suddenly stung the corners of Catherine's large, almond-shaped eyes.

'Oh come, come,' Anja placed a comforting arm around her shoulders, 'surely it is not an occasion for sadness?'

'No, no, it's just...' Catherine strived to contain herself, 'well, you can't imagine how frustrating it's been these last years - not knowing anything about myself, trying to remember some small detail that might begin to unravel the mystery of who I am and getting nowhere. It seems at times as if my entire existence has been spent... how can I describe it... like walking in slow motion like a camel, climbing vast hillocks of yellow sand only to be confronted with yet more, and not a mirage in sight. You know, there are moments when I wake from a dream that hasn't quite ended and catch a small part of what might have once been my life.' She shook her head. 'I cook every day and wonder under whose tuition I learnt. I wonder how I acquired a knowledge of architecture, of books, the songs that I sing, of geography. Have I visited the places that seem so familiar to me, Madagascar, Brazil, the Outer Hebrides or simply been a mental traveller? How do I know that Tamarisk bushes are not just mustardy in colour but full of gold and butter and champagne? How do I know that there is no such thing as a barren desert, that their immenseness simply forces people to recognise their own insignificance and that's why they are so often denounced. Their barrenness comes from within.'

'Then you know more than most already.'

'It's not the same. You know, I can smell the scent of bristlecone pines, see each detail of a panamint daisy, visualise the circus beetles dragging their loads through the sands and pupfish wading through salt waters, but I can't see *me*. I know of events from recent past and ancient histories. I can recognise characters on a screen, voices on a radio, but I know nothing of myself. Do I have any family? Can I ride a bicycle? If I dived into the Adriatic Sea would I drown or can I swim? Do I have any undiscovered talents? Who has fooled me with their lies? Who have I loved? Who made me weep? Whose body has entered mine?' She thought of *him*. Sex with him had been something solely for the night, something vampirical, to be kept in a box and raised from the dead in surreptitious moments of darkness. They had been the worst of lovers. 'And what's more, I don't know what scares me the most, not knowing who I am or the fear of discovery.'

Hilda entered the room. 'Where's the remote control? My programme's just starting. Have you put it in the wrong place again?'

'No Hilda it is just where you left it on the table.' The old lady shuffled off. 'She becomes more like her son every day or is it the other way around? He too is always accusing me of putting things in the wrong places, especially when he trips over something. He's accused me of it so often that yesterday I doodled him with a quiff between his legs and pubes on his forehead.'

Catherine and Rosy laughed. Catherine added, 'Perhaps relationships are always like that, like a game of Blind Man's Buff, tripping over the same old obstacles, groping about in the dark, not for flesh to tease but simply to find your way through all the crap that comes with two people inhabiting the same space?'

'*Ja* it is.'

'No,' Rosy cast a reproachful look at Anja, 'no it doesn't have to be. You should leave the farm, find what it is you're looking for.'

'I know, but I haven't the courage. I don't have a lot of money or a proper job, my life is at the farm. God, I despise my cowardice. I've just let it drag on.' She mused. 'People should leave each other quickly shouldn't they, always jolly tars until they're buried in the foam.'

'*Und was ist **tars**?* What does that mean? I wish you would both speak more simply. You must remember I am not speaking in my mother tongue.'

'Oh just ignore her.'

'*Na Ja, sehr schön,* very nice I'm sure.'

'Anyway,' Catherine continued, 'yesterday, when I saw this man John Smith on the television screen there was some recognition, though what exactly I don't know. And I suddenly wondered why he had painted me and if he knows anything about me, whether he could fit any of the pieces together - that maybe he and I had some connection. Despite all my grievances I have the feeling that I once loved someone so deeply that we hit oil.'

'*Ja,* but maybe it is just a coincidence that he paints this woman like you. I would hate for you to get your hopes up only to find that you are chasing false dreams.'

'Never mind dreams,' the old lady entered the room suddenly, shaking her stick, 'you should all be out there looking for Twinkletoes. I can't find him. I wrapped him in a newspaper when he died. Don't read them myself but Albert likes to keep up with the politics.'

'*Um Gottes willen*! Albert's been dead for years Hilda.'

'Never could see the point myself. Nothing ever changes wherever you put your cross. All the same, politicians, only interested in feathering their own nests.'

Catherine resisted the urge to laugh at the unintended pun.

'I wrapped him up in an article about the recession or something. Albert would know.' She pointed her crutch at Anja. 'Ask him when he gets home from work. He might remember where I put it.'

'Albert's dead Hilda. Don't you remember?'

Rosy made an effort to lighten the conversation. 'Recession eh? Do you know what the difference is between a recession and a depression? A recession is when *you* lose *your* job, a depression is when *I* lose *mine.*'

'That's an old one.' Hilda's whiskers trembled. 'I do miss him.'

Catherine wondered if she was referring to Albert or the bird. She almost whispered, 'I'm aware that I may be barking up the wrong tree as far as the painting is concerned, but I need to find out. I just don't quite know how to go about it?'

Anja stood up. 'We need to go to the beach. I always think better when at the beach. I can't think here with talk of marmite and Albert and dead birds.'

The beach was still wet and hard from the sea's recent retreat and modest waves arched and broke soothingly onto the shore. The children were inevitably drawn to it and after a moment the elder two boys plunged into its depths with a steely bravado. Anja immediately began erecting deck chairs and wind breakers and distributing beach towels. Catherine thought again of the mysterious John Smith and momentarily wished she was alone. Her thoughts were obscured by the presence of other voices and she wanted to consider them with clarity. She watched, feeling herself reluctantly drawn in, painted once more into another vibrant canvas. The sight of a radio spilling from Rosy's rucksack depressed her. She settled uneasily onto a towel grateful at least that commercialism had not yet spoilt their surroundings - no pier, no promenade, no jingling, phlegmatic donkeys tyrannised by over-sized children. Anja stood above her, impatience displayed by the angle of her hip.

'I have seen this look before. It is no use going into your shell if you want us to help.'

Catherine smiled affectionately. 'You're absolutely right.' She watched the children. The youngest two were collecting pebbles and shells, their chief pride of which was etched with shapes of presumed fossil plants. They exhibited these generously, ignored only by the two boys who, now tired of swimming, sat apart, silent and contemplative, throwing pebbles into foam and rebuking attempts at interaction.

Emily ran to her mother with the rosy glow of an angel bringing good tidings. 'Look,' she said, 'I found it in the seaweed.' It was a green bottle of the old-fashioned variety and for a brief moment Catherine felt a hint of a recollection but then it was gone. 'One green bottle,' Emily sang, 'hanging on a wall.'

Rosy took a book out of her bag in an attempt to dispel the sobriety. 'Anja, I'd almost forgotten, I got this especially for you.' She handed Anja the book she had bought at the local joke shop. 'I knew you'd like it as soon as I saw it.'

Anja read the title in her thick accent. '*Vot Men Can Tell You About Sex*.' She turned the book over and read the back cover. 'Over one thousand men interviewed. This book took twelve months to compile. The *Kama Sutra* is child's play compared to this edition. All I can say is WHERE ARE ZEESE MEN?' She opened the book to discover empty pages and threw it down in disgust. 'There is nothing inside. You must have bought a faulty copy. We should send it back to the publisher. It's a disgrace.'

Rosy and Catherine began laughing.

'That's the joke,' Rosy expanded, 'there is nothing.'

She and Catherine exchanged glances. The faint brackets around Catherine's mouth deepened to accommodate her small, regular teeth in a smile.

'The indication being,' Rosy continued, 'that they, *men* I mean, know nothing... about sex that is.' She glanced despairingly at Catherine. 'The joke sort of gets lost in the translation. I thought it was very funny the first time I read it.'

'*Accch Ja*, I get it. Very funny. The famous British humour. Oh, *Ja, Ja,* very funny, *sehr schön*.' She began to laugh hysterically.

Catherine said, 'Actually it's a bit sad if you think about it.'

'Well,' Rosy opened the bottle of wine she'd brought with her, 'men must know something about sex otherwise Anja wouldn't have six children.'

'Bulls impregnate cows,' Catherine replied, 'but it doesn't mean they know anything about foreplay.'

Anja laughed even louder. '*Acch,* bulls, now that *is* funny. Very funny!'

'If you think that's funny,' said Catherine, 'then try milking one.'

Tears ran down Anja's cheeks. 'Milking one, oh, very good, very good, *sehr schön.*'

'You see,' Rosy smiled broadly at Catherine and Anja, 'it's not a lack of humour that the Germans suffer from, it's delayed reaction. No one realizes what a responsive audience they can be because by the time they start laughing, everyone else has gone home!'

'*Acch,* very bloody funny.'

'The problem with men is,' Rosy continued, 'you can't live with them and you can't live without them.'

'Speak for yourself,' said Catherine,

'Personally I couldn't imagine life without a man,' Rosy said. 'I couldn't manage without the sex. Even the kind implied in that book.'

'Nymphomaniac,' Anja said affectionately, 'personally I think all men are shits, especially mine, now he's a real *scheißkerl.*'

Catherine was pleased now that she had come. She tossed the sand between her pale toes and regarded the sea which conjured a torrent of words and images all of which were now hopeful. When she thought of John

Smith she was conscious of a distorted image of happiness that lay almost tangible somewhere amongst the rocks and seaweed and shadows. She breathed the salty vapours consciously, filling her lungs.

'We need to devise a plan,' Rosy continued. 'We have to work out a way for Catherine to meet this John Smith and then she'll find out one way or another whether there's anything in it. We know his exhibition is in London at the moment at the Tate Modern, and it mentioned at the end of the show that he's giving a presentation. Catherine simply has to turn up and if he responds to her then she'll know and if he doesn't then, well, at least you'll know it was just a coincidence.'

'But how,' Catherine felt a wave of despair returning, 'how can I possibly get to London? And what about Emily?'

'Easy, Anja will have Emily and Lucy for a while and I will drive you there. Sending you to London on your own would be like sending a lamb to the slaughter. We can be there and back in the space of a day. No one will even know you're gone.'

'And if they did you could say that you have been to yoga. This is an anagram of *Goya* so you would be telling no proper lies.'

'Very good Anja.'

'*Ja*, not bad eh, considering English is not my native tongue.'

'I have an inspired idea too,' Rosy said, 'I have that black gypsy skirt and lace top - you know, like the dress the Duchess of Alba wears in Goya's famous painting of the *Black Duchess*. I'll alter the measurements and we'll crimp your hair so that you look exactly like her. If that doesn't make an impact then I don't know what will.'

'Oh I don't know. The whole idea's a bit mad. Maybe I should forget the whole thing.' Catherine cast her eyes out to sea. 'Or else send him a message in the bottle and hope one day he discovers it'

'You'd be better off e-mailing.'

'Not as romantic.'

'*Acchh Ja* romance. Where did that ever get anyone?'

'Catherine, what have you got to lose? This may be your one chance to find out who you are and if not, well, at least it will have been an adventure.'

Catherine knew Rosy was right. In the breeze of memory she felt she had once been truly happy. Was it possible to recreate happiness? Perhaps thoughts of retrieving it were best locked in a deep chest weighted with barnacle and sunk to irretrievable depths so as not to be mistaken for a possibility. The problem was that, when the light was right and the sea was calm, just as it was now, she would snatch brief glimpses of it from the cliff edge glimmering beneath the surface spume.

*

High above on the cliff top, *he* observed the scene. She could not see him yet something subliminal told her he was there, that his sun-weathered face looked older with each jealous thought. In her mind's eye she could imagine his silent, narrow-eyed concentration, his features bitten by a frost of contempt that seemed all-pervading rather than denoting any singularity of purpose. She could imagine too his tattered appearance as careless as a vagrant's, his manner measured and deliberate, performing with ease and lack of conscience, the role of predator. For a large man he would be surprisingly noiseless and would know instinctively where to stand to remain concealed. From his vantage point he would watch the women and children on the beach who would seem small and vulnerable next to the infinite expanse of the sea which appeared almost too calm, too uncommunicative. He would be momentarily gripped by his fear of it. He would wipe his forehead with the lower part of his T-shirt, revealing a body that was used to physical labour and note with alarm the clouds on the horizon, ebonized almost by his censure. The party on the beach would exhibit no concern yet it would seem to him that the sea, presently mute, barely licking at the bare toes of those small, squealing bodies, could, at any time change its mood dramatically, rising in dissension to engulf them all. Thoughts of losing her would addle his mind. He would agonise with these thoughts for some time, his large, masculine shape subdued both by fear and posture. When he next looked the beach would be unpeopled, the sea ever-tranquil and the dark clouds blanched and dovish, like emblems of peace.

*

CHAPTER 5

The sepia-coloured pages remained blank. This was unlike him. John Smith lit a cigarette. What prevented his thoughts from spilling onto the pages in endless spirals? Was it the humming of the fridge in the kitchen, the occasional car horn from the road, the mocking church bells as they struck yet another fruitless hour? Or was it the woman who remained locked in his head along with the words, like a ship in a bottle, only to be obtained by breaking the glass? He glanced at the sketch he had done of her in preparation for the painting. After all this time he still wanted to throw himself into her puddles. He must stop being morbid before his nightshade tones soured the milk and spooked the cats. He picked up his mobile and cancelled the date he had made for that evening with the woman introduced to him through his agent. He knew it would prove pointless - transient moments of sexual healing... But the cold light of day had already cast too many shadows. In any case it was not worth it, he thought. He might as well be using that time-honoured method of self-abuse, you know, the one that's supposed to affect your eyesight. If those experiences had taught him anything at all it was that sex was not just about self-gratification, not just for documentary purposes.

He half-heartedly studied the empty pages again and gave up. The article was for the Museum of Modern Art in New York and needed to be finished by the end of the week. He sighed. He would sit there till darkness came and inspiration with it. Funny how his thoughts seemed to grow more readily in the darkness - like the roots of a tree. He picked up the sketch of his Duchess of Alba, refined, modified to his personal specifications. She stared back at him. She almost appeared to have a life of her own. What provoked that look of singular animation in her face? Was she caught up in the subtle mutations of falling in love? He laughed out loud. He really was going mad. He screwed up the paper and threw it to the far end of the studio. Enough was enough.

There was a knock at the door. It was his agent Griffin. An irritating name he thought, like Ptolemy or Montague. He liked the simplicity of his own.

'Have you finished the article yet?'

'If you'd piss off I might stand a chance.'

His agent laughed good-naturedly. 'Well make it good. You know the American buyers will be reading it. Make it big in New York and we're set up for life. As the song goes, *"If you can make it there, you'll make it anywhere…"* They love this idea of Goya being reincarnated. It's his vision of doom and gloom they're caught up in. So think macabre, think deep abyss of human misery, think…'

'What if I'm not feeling particularly *deep abyss*?'

'You always are lately. And anyway, just look in the papers.' He threw down the newspaper he had been carrying. 'Between natural disasters there's the everyday run of the mill shootings, stabbings, rape and other assorted felonies - the list is endless. In fact it's amazing that people just don't emigrate.'

'What, and give up the good life.'

Griffin laughed. 'That's the spirit. You're never short of the old repartee, I'll give you that. So don't let me down. Baffle them with some of that bullshit about you and the Duchess of Alba, the Yanks will love that.' He studied some of the paintings in the studio and, noticing the discarded sketch, picked it up and unravelled it. 'Weren't you supposed to be going on a date tonight? You know, red head, legs up to her arm pits... ring any bells?'

'I cancelled.'

'Are you mad?'

'Very likely. Anyone who has you for an agent has got to be seriously deranged.'

'She's gorgeous.'

'And probably very nice, which is why she deserves better than me. Anyway, I'd probably only end up hurting her, though not on purpose - more like a scorpion that can't feel except through the sting in its tail. No, no, best just to steal her image till I'm alone in bed and can harmlessly manipulate her through all the positions my licentious imaginings can create. It seems the only creativity I can conjure up these days, by sleight of hand, that spurting libido waste. And what a waste.'

'Christ, you need to get laid.'

'You're probably right.'

'It's supposed to be a good thing you know, this fame thing. It might only last the proverbial fifteen minutes so make the most of it. It's supposed to make you happy.'

'Well yeah, just look around you.' He gestured to the paintings, dramatic chiaroscuro everywhere, dense paint applied in manic sweeps, screaming people tormented and tormenting, their black-socketed eyes blazing red here and there as if streaked with blood, ugly demons with cloven-hooves and vast, ebony torsos which seemed, he thought, to bear the culpability of mankind along with its evil. 'Such ghastly extremities of ugliness that you can almost hear the muffled canting of lost souls that Goya's deafness disallowed, amongst them my own. Having sold my soul to the devil what do you expect. I'm painting a world devoid of compassion. And you want happiness? Go and manage Rolf Harris.'

Griffin glanced at the sketch in his hand. 'This mood doesn't have anything to do with her by any chance?'

'Maybe.' He shrugged. 'I expect so. It's four years, four months and four days since I lost her - them. Just lately her face materialises everywhere.'

'Oh I see.'

'Do you?'

'Well, yes…but you know John, that's a long time. And giving up a date with a real, live woman won't bring her back. *Real* and *live* being the operative words incidentally. And you seemed okay. I don't quite understand…Why now John?'

'Hell, I don't know. Why do we feel the things we feel Griff?' He shrugged. 'Why do we love the people we do? It's none the clearer after aeons of orgasms and indeterminable periods of giddy giggles. Oh God yes, I remember, there were so many of those. I would hold her waist, that egg timer spilling rapture through my fingers, our vibrations quaking with happiness. And as we beat together in the candlelit studio, the molten cortex lapping in our ears, it seemed at times like life began and ended there.'

'YEAH YEAH, that's it.'

'What? What's it? What are you talking about?'

'That's exactly the kind of mawkish nonsense that the Yanks will love.' He held the empty notebook in outstretched arms. 'Quick get it down.'

'Christ, you're just abundant with inherent sensitivity aren't you?'

'We can but try,' he sighed. 'My girlfriend thinks I'm charming.'

'Who? Oh, the one with the inflated lips and chest who's permanently clad in leopard-skin? Yeah, right, I can imagine what *her* definition of charming is - someone who says please beforehand, thanks afterwards and takes the weight on his elbows.'

After Griffin had gone, unable to shake off his melancholy, John decided to take a walk. Unintentionally he found himself nearing the Thames and he quickened his pace to stave off the evening chill. It was an ugly stretch of water, particularly at night and tonight was not a good night for him to reflect on its character. WOMAN MISSING, PRESUMED DROWNED, the headlines had stated those four, long years ago. Like a scene from a Daphne du Maurier novel. It began to rain, tears of rain, he thought, pouring down from rank skies, seemingly drowning the moon, which, laden with purple melancholy, dropped its heavy, beaming globe momentarily onto the water's surface until, slowly and painfully, like a sinking ship, it appeared submerged completely. It was, he thought, a great night for lunacy. Soon no doubt the moon would return to coin the sky and the man inside it would *"laugh and laugh to see such fun."* He had to snap out of this. The Thames did not help. He knelt there on its bank like Narcissus, praying for some small, flickering of ancient wisdom, a faint, lapping reassurance of reflected beauty, belonging not to him but to the world at large, and it stared back offering nothing. Water, normally symbolic of life and potency had turned tail and stank of death.

The Thames was so supremely ugly that it seemed to pull him into its depths, not to swim but to drown. It seemed to him like a giant sewer, sweeping up a refuse of lost dreams. He wondered how many lives it had claimed. He remembered having thought the same of the sea after Maria's drowning. He had driven to the place where it had happened, where she had sailed out in a boat and never returned. How lonely she must have been in her death, how frightened. The sea had appeared at that moment so ugly that the only way to rid himself of its gracelessness had seemed to be to jump into its lugubrious depths, to souse in its miserable belly so that he could be spared the malice of its face. He had seen their child there too, waiting just below the surface to be born. He had felt that, had he waded in he could pull back the bellyskin of water and deliver him or her, like Julius Caesar before him, into life's arena. Deep beneath the waves his baby seemed to smile and raise its hand like a gay flag. For a moment happiness had flared up in him like a tall-tailed wick. Then the image had disappeared and the light had flickered out.

He rose and turned in the direction of his studio. He felt cold then and a violent urge to be sick. He bent his head. People walked past, turning away. He supposed that London was full of vomiting people like him. They were probably as indigenous a part of the scenery as London's Beefeaters or the Queen's Guards and not one of them bore more or less significance than the London fog which frequently hung in limp clusters over its ancient buildings, or the pigeons in Trafalgar Square which ate greedily and excreted their luck for free.

CHAPTER 6

Catherine awoke alone yet something intuitive told her she was not. She left the house stealthily, like a practiced thief and made her way once more toward the coastal path. She found it easier this time to walk away and easier to resist the temptation to look back. Although they were early Anja was already waiting at the gate of the cottage like an anxious mother hen motioning to Rosy who had her head under the bonnet of her car.

'She is very moody today. First she leaves her lights on last night and the battery is now flat and secondly she discovers that little boy she was seeing already has three other girlfriends. *Na Ja.*'

'Oh dear.' Catherine took off the rucksack with Emily's things in it and watched her daughter run triumphantly into the house where she was met by Lucy and Anja's children.

Rosy raised her hand from beneath the bonnet of the car. 'It's true what they say - if it has tyres or testicles you'll have problems with it sooner or later.'

Anja laughed her throaty laugh. 'Come, come, you must change before it is time to leave for London. I have made some changes to the skirt but the top I think will fit you very well.'

'You know, I'm not sure that this is such a good idea. It will probably prove to be an entirely fruitless journey.'

'*Quatsch*, nonsense, you must go. What is the alternative? To stay in that gloomy house for the rest of your days? Look...' She held Catherine's shoulders firmly, her corn-flecked eyes filling suddenly with tears, 'you know, my daughter asked me the other week why I talk differently to the other mothers. I woke up in the night thinking about it. Or maybe it was my husband's snoring that woke me. It's like sleeping in a pig stable with him.'

'Pig *sty*.'

'*Aachh* whatever! Anyway, I tell her about Germany and how I come here and I show her pictures of all her relatives back home. Then I think about you and how you know nothing of your past and I think how terrible this must be for you, how alone you must sometimes feel with so little affection.'

'It's not so bad really. I have Emily.'

'I know how it must be. The only time my husband shows any affection, meagre affection though it may be is at night. One kiss before and one after. Well, I say kiss, it is really no more than a pick.'

'Peck.'

'*Acchh*, pick, peck, what's the difference. I expect he saves the real stuff, the deep throat stuff I mean, for that tart he is sleeping with.'

'He's having an affair?'

'*Acchh Ja*, he is *always* having an affair though he thinks I don't know.'

'Then you should divorce him, unless you still love him of course?'

'*Acchh*, what's love got to do with it? We have more than love to consider.' Anja led the way back to the house. 'We have children, a mortgage, joint friends, a hamster, not to mention the crazy mother-in law.' She looked around lest Hilda should appear. 'Love is really the last consideration. And,' she paused, 'I have the life that I want, you and Rosy, my children, my art. But, don't you see,' she sighed heavily, 'my tears are not for my marriage but for *you* my lost friend, living a lie. I fear for what it will do to you. You must find a way to discover yourself before it is too late.' Emotion rose in Catherine's throat moistening her almond-shaped eyes.

'Damn car.' Rosy joined them. 'What are you both talking about so seriously?'

'*Acchh,* life, marriage and divorce... you know.'

'The thing about marriage is,' Catherine interjected, 'how do you know when enough is enough, when to throw in the towel as they say? There has to be a point of realization when you know you can't go on but how do you recognise it, and more to the point, how do you act upon it?'

Anja shrugged. 'It is easy my friend, you just follow your heart.'

'With me it was easy,' Rosy smiled, 'all to do with condoms.'

'*Achhhh Quatsch,* condoms! Condoms ended your marriage?'

'Wouldn't it have been easier just to change contraceptive?'

'Fools, no.' Rosy began to use the curling tongs on Catherine's hair. 'It was after I'd had Lucy. You know how exhausting it can be, well, you especially Anja with all your brood, never getting a proper night's sleep. And Lucy was a terrible baby, screaming to be fed every two hours. He *never once* offered to fetch her. But it didn't stop him wanting sex. And in the middle of it the baby would cry and I'd think I've got to go to her but he'd just keep going till he was finished. There was no grace to it. Then he'd roll over and fall asleep and I'd be left to struggle out of bed like a zombie. "I'm coming," I'd say. I only ever seemed to say it in connection with the baby in those days. And I'd circumvent the bed frame, the strewn clothing and the frustrated *bundle* of male sex that he'd thrown on the floor, trapped like goldfish in their latex bowl. Women are such victims it seemed to say.'

'But I don't quite see…'

'After I'd fed the baby I couldn't sleep for ages. *"Dispose of hygienically and thoughtfully,"* it had said on the packet. He obviously hadn't read it. But then, tidying up was my job. Man's job to fill it up, women's job to tidy it up. I used to lie in the darkness, eyes fixed on the ceiling following the bead of light from the landing. Too tired and too frustrated for sleep. Strange how he never woke up when the baby cried. I used to wonder if the sound of batteries would wake him. *Always ready ever ready.* Then I'd close my eyes and think of Imran Khan.'

'Imran Khan?'

Anja sighed. '"*Es gibt Sonne genug, es gibt Acke genug. Hätten wir nur Liebe genug*"'

'What's that?'

'Sit still, I want to do your make-up. I repeat the words of, oh, I can't remember who. It means there is sun enough, there is acre enough, if only there was enough love.'

'There ought to be.'

'*Ja*, there ought to be but there is not. You know, if you were not both going off to London now I would suggest we get drunk. As pissed as frogs.'

'Newts.'

'*Acchh, Ja, votever*. There!' She pulled the sash around Catherine's waist. 'Finished. And who could possibly say that you are not the Duchess herself.'

'Incredible. You look more like the Duchess of Alba than she did.'

Catherine stood and turned to the mirror. Even she was stunned by the transformation. The subtle blusher animated her flawless, pale skin and her crimped, ebony, *Maja* hair cascaded onto a filigree of sheer black lace. A red sash was secured tightly around her waist, exaggerating the curve of her slender hips which were dressed in a long, black gypsy skirt. She felt the eternal spirit of the Duchess of Alba eddy through her veins. Before the mirror she pointed her finger downward and echoed the immortal words, "*Solo Goya*," Only Goya, that could be determined in the painting *Black Duchess*. Many had believed these were not the Duchess's true sentiments and that their inclusion was indicative only of the desperate and unrequited obsession of an ageing Goya. No one would ever know the truth.

At that moment Hilda entered the room on two crutches. 'I've lost my leg.'

'Again Hilda? This is becoming a habit. One moment and I will look for it for you.'

Catherine wondered if she would be the same when she was old, lost and forgetful. She imagined herself, whiskers growing longer each year with every new trial - leaking radiators, ants in the kitchen, a dead Twinkletoes. Had Hilda ever bothered to pluck them? Had Albert ever complained about them when he was alive? Or had the venom of their arguments long since denied such intimacy? She suddenly felt disproportionately sorry for the old lady, for deceased Albert and the dead bird. It strengthened her resolve that she was doing the right thing. Maybe there was something out there for her to discover, or maybe after all happiness was just an illusion - like the itch of an amputated limb. But she had to try to find out.

'We must go.'

Anja kissed Catherine lightly on the cheek. 'Good luck and don't worry about Emily and Lucy. I will take good care of them both.'

The drive took several hours but Catherine hardly registered its inconvenience. She felt like a child on her first journey, engulfed by the excitement of her anticipated arrival. She watched with fascination as the landscape changed and even the widening roads, fat with traffic could not diffuse her animation. It was as if, for the first time she recognised the enormity of the world and with it, the possibility of change, of a new life. She listened as Rosy chatted, absorbing only half of the content, disinterested yet comforted by her friend's garrulousness. It was only when they approached central London, noisy, congested and filled with hurried figures all seemingly purposed of destination, that fear began to resurface and she considered for the first time the possibility of disappointment.

'Oh, don't worry,' Rosy anticipated her friend's anxiety, 'you have nothing to lose and everything to gain.'

'You don't think I'll be making too much of an exhibition of myself.'

'Isn't that what art's all about - exhibition?' She smiled. 'Come on Duchess, let's go before you change your mind.

I haven't driven all this way for nothing. If nothing else you will see your portrait in the flesh so to speak.'

'I suppose you're right.'

'I'll get you as close to the gallery as possible. Then I'll have to leave you while I park the car. I'll catch up with you later. Whatever you do, don't leave the gallery.'

Catherine's panic returned. 'I'd rather come with you. Then we can arrive together.'

'It might take me some time to park and it looks like rain. We don't want to ruin your hair and dress.'

'It really doesn't matter.'

'Look this is a good spot to drop you off. Just follow the signs. You can't miss the building. It's the old Bankside Power Station, ugly building like a red bricked coffin with a huge square chimney in the middle of it.'

'Very encouraging. Makes it sound like I'm going to a funeral. Hope that's not an omen.'

'You're a hop, skip and a jump away. Quick, I need to move on.'

The car behind them sounded its horn. Catherine hurriedly scrambled from the vehicle to the footpath and watched in panic as Rosy disappeared into the distance. For a few moments she felt rooted to the spot like an animal caught in the intoxicating glare of headlights. Then she turned and began to walk, slowly and carefully, conscious of the stares of passers-by. In this city so vast and impersonal, she felt they could sense the fear of the dispossessed. She felt small and abandoned in a strange world of gargantuan noise and space and stature. She did not understand that she bewitched all those who cast eyes on her that day, that her sphinxian beauty set her apart from all the others with their high street legs and sleek, metropolitan hair.

It began to rain lightly and the rain seemed to exacerbate her self-doubt. Despite her fondness for Rosy she wished she was with someone older who could watch out for her, a mother, or even an elderly aunt. When she had first awoken from her coma during labour the midwife had helped her come to terms with her ordeal. She had seemed so wise. She had laughed when Catherine had told her this and said that if she gave that impression it was probably because she kept quiet and that her quietness was due to the fact that she really had no answers. "Life is something of a mish mash," she had said, "but I do believe in God." At least she had had that.

CHAPTER 7

John Smith arrived at the Tate Modern early, eager for some distraction before his lecture. He did not have to travel far. The great Turbine Hall was dominated by two vast exhibits, *The Towers* and the spider *Maman,* both sculptures by artist Louise Bourgeois. Both exhibits were composed mainly of steel which at first seemed to him their only correlation. He climbed to the top of the towers and sat for respite on the seat provided on the platform where large mirrors were positioned. It was then that the towers with their phallic shafts and spiral stairways began to feel reminiscent of mythologies, maidens locked in captive towers releasing their lengthy hair, spinning webs of cloth as their only distraction. He felt a discomfort, looking at himself in the mirrors and assumed this was because of their narcissistic implications. Too much time for reflection was not healthy. Dissecting one's appearance was futile and meditating over past behaviour even more ineffectual. One seldom discovered the truth, only versions of it, sanitised over the years by shame and regret. He read the captions.

And moving through a mirror clear
That hangs before her all the year
Shadows of the world appear

The Lady of Shalott from Arthurian legend had been held in captivity in a tower, left weaving like a spider,

Weaving by night and day
A magic web with colours gay.

Her curse proffered in the poem by Lord Tennyson had been that she hadn't been able to see the world except through the mirror. And here at the top of the Bourgeois tower were mirrors, placed strategically for those, like him, who were seduced into a web of introspection and didn't necessarily like what they saw. But she was dead and he was alive and he had to accept that and purge himself of these thoughts. Life was for the living. He'd been a fool. But not any more. Ding dong the Duchess of Alba was dead. The tin man had at last found some brains.

He walked toward his gallery. He was due to begin his lecture in ten minutes with the usual question time. He felt no guilt at his deception. Christ if people were gullible enough to believe that he was Goya reincarnated then they were beyond help anyway. The more he saw of people the less he felt he understood them. But then people were seldom transparent. Most of them he supposed, like Seurat's paintings, were made up of zillions of dots which were only black and white when examined under a microscope. Stand back far enough and we were all grey, grey like the earl in the tea caddy. What type of people would give him the time of day? The type who no doubt believed what they read in the newspapers, watched reality shows, bought useless products that were sold to them by slick advertising companies. The extent of human naivety was astonishing. But perhaps he was being too cynical. Perhaps all you ever saw of others were the images they chose to contrive, like reflections from a hall of mirrors, fat ones, thin ones, elongated Modigliani faces, all real and yet all so bloody bizarre. And he had been the most idiotic of all. Talk about chasing false Gods. He had so often accused others of that - money, fame and all those things that people believed would enrich their lives - greedy, consumerist things. But at least they were tangible, they were real, they existed. Unlike his Duchess. He laughed out loud at his own foolishness. But his sanity had returned. He was now free of her.

His lecture was over-subscribed and this amused him. Five minutes ago it seemed, he'd been anonymous and now his claims of another identity had gained him a somewhat reluctant celebrity. He was no more accomplished at painting now than he had been a year before but his work had been given a certain provenance that made the difference between being commercially successful and a talented artist starving in his garret. After he'd shown slides of his work and discussed technique hands began to raise.

'Yes, the lady in lavender.'

'I'd like to know,' she began in a lazy Scottish accent, 'are you hoping to achieve immortality by claiming to be Goya?'

'No, as Woody Allen said, "I'd like to achieve that by not dying."' Laughter ensued.

'Next question.'

'As a painter what do you think of Conceptual Art?'

This had to be an art student. 'That it should remain just that. Unfortunately for the general public some artists feel a need to follow the concept through so that we're obliged to view a glass of water on a shelf in a gallery of all places and refer to it as *An Oak Tree*.'

'The Chapman brothers were strongly influenced by Goya.' The man speaking looked suspiciously like Dinos Chapman himself. 'What do you think of their work?'

'Grown men playing with dolls. What more is there to say.'

'Duchamp put a *urinal*, a ready-made into a gallery and called it *Fountain*. Some who visit it here at the Tate Modern say it has a spiritual resonance. What do you think?' (Serious-looking gentleman in a suit.)

'It's a urinal. You piss in it. It's a piece of piss.' (More laughter.)

'Who's your favourite artist?'

'Me.'

'Most art critics have given you bad press because of your claims. What do you think of art critics generally?'

'Morons put on this earth just to make up the numbers. There isn't one with a creative bone in his or her body.'

'Do you think your...um, Goya's work, still has relevance today?'

'How can it not? Goya's work is cross-cultural and ahistorical; wholly applicable to contemporary times. Goya was referred to as the Father of Modern Art long before Cezanne. And who in the present world could not identify with those cynical images, particularly the *Disasters of War Series* and the *Caprichos*, whose images of torment, suffering and carnage along with the hypocrisies and perversions of politicians and other quasi pillars of society have become part of the staple diet of broadcasting? Globalisation has made the world a smaller place; suffering and hypocrisy are now considered fair play in the world of entertainment, wars are enacted on television screens in the comfort of your own home. And not the wars in films but REAL blood and guts wars with living and dying and dead people. All this while you sip your wine and eat your popcorn in the comfort of your armchair.'

There was some dissent in the audience, a student trying to impress his classmates no doubt. 'What do you think of contemporary Britain then? It must differ vastly from nineteenth-century Spain.' (giggles)

'Not at all. As far as I'm concerned, nineteenth-century Spain has nothing on the impenetrable denseness of the recent British government which led its country, albeit reluctantly, into war with the same Napoleonic pretexts of liberating the oppressed. No difference really, just different people who die, mostly innocents whose images scream out tragically from the pages of daily newspapers. And these I document, not with the same professional detachment of Nash or Nevinson I'm afraid. But a lack of emotion in Goya's work has never been a criticism has it? In this sense I can claim to be an emotional man.'

He continued to answer all the questions. Yes art had changed for the worst in many respects. Of course there was now an inexhaustive expanse of artistic expression such as installations, GPS drawing, conceptual and performance art. But what did this mean to a real painter? Despite endless predictions of its imminent demise, painting had survived and flourished. What other art form could compete with the pure, unadulterated pleasure of painting? Only other painters understood the joy involved in the physicality of the process, those tactile tubes of colour oozing their presence, motioning the brush into sweeping caresses or violently smeared blades of impasto. What did the Chapman brothers understand of this? No, art had not advanced with time. Nor human nature come to that.

It was then that a voice broke out from the crowd, loud and contemptuous, breaking the relative calm.

'IMPOSTOR!'

The man stood, small and compelling, his darkness exotic amidst the pale insipidness of the crowd. His frown expressed an obstinacy that refused to be compromised. He stared beleaguered at John Smith, as though he was facing the enemy across a battlefield, someone who he knew not, but had determined to conquer at any price, not out of malice but in order to remain. 'You are an impostor,' he repeated, his voice belying his stature, booming like a fabled giant. 'You have written that you had an illegitimate child with the Duchess of Alba. You claim to have painted them and say that this painting was stolen only to be brought to England. How can you know such things about Goya and Alba? I have spent my entire life studying them. I have lived on the soil they lived, smelt the earth where they trod. I know them as I know my brothers and sisters, my mother, my departed father. I have followed their trail. The things I have uncovered belong to me, have been procured by sweat and tears, years of exhaustive research. And *you*, somehow you claim to know these things, magically, as though you have consulted some oracle, as though the Gods have somehow favoured you by whispering the secrets of centuries. I want to know how you have come by these ideas?' He paused long enough only to swallow his distaste and inhale his next vitriolic breath. 'It is true that you have Goya's fire in your work, some of his passion, his genius. There are similarities I agree. But why do you make up these stories? I am not just an art historian. Goya and his mistress have been my life. Why do you torment me with your foolish claims? Do you wish to confuse the face of history? It is only a pity that the Spanish Inquisition no longer exists. You and your lies. They would hang you from the nearest tree, they would slit you from top to bottom, they would...'

'Now just a minute...' As amused as he was by this outburst John Smith thought it somewhat histrionic. He had expected some amusement from his audience, disbelief certainly, ridicule even, but this man was genuinely aggrieved, as though he privately supposed the claims credible enough to warrant serious explanation.

Before he could conjure his usual witty retort he was distracted further by the response of the crowd to some further inexpectation. Curious, he turned to observe the subject of their diversion and it was then that he saw her. Perhaps because of his new resolve to forget her, which had been strengthened in some inexplicable way by those moments of reflection at the top of the Bourgeois towers, the sight of her met him first with an unexpected sense of alarm that quickly transposed to sadness. Could this really be her? Could she have managed her life these last years without being eclipsed by the shadow that his misery had surely cast?

'Maria,' he spoke her name quietly, 'Maria.'

The woman did not respond but moved across the gallery, seemingly oblivious to the crowd who turned to watch her, captivated by her presence. She walked quietly and resolutely and did not stop until she stood before the painting of the Duchess of Alba. It hung on the far wall of the white cube gallery room, no heavily patterned background to distract from its enveloping aura. The woman's hair was wet from a rainfall, a mass of unravelling curls which caused the exquisite lace of her blouse to embrace her skin with ever-greater urgency. If anything the wetness had enhanced her beauty. Her fragility and that of the lace married together like cleverly placed works of art, the red, full lips conspicuous in the milky serenity of her damp face. She stood, transfixed by her mirror image, her form and features complementing those of the woman imprisoned within the frame, as if through the formal devices of the painting.

'Maria.' Words formed in the space between his dry lips but were quickly swallowed up. He moved toward her, his audience temporarily forgotten. At last he recovered his voice. 'It can't be. Surely not. Maria, is that you?'

For the first time she turned toward him and he marvelled at the familiarity of her beautiful face.

'Do you know me?' The voice was hers, nervous and quizzical in tone yet entirely her own.

'Of course I do. You know I do. But I thought…' His voice strained under the weight of emotion, his words barely audible, 'I thought you were dead.'

She seemed about to speak when a voice broke the promise of intimacy.

'IMPOSTOR!' The small, dark man began yelling once more from the crowd. 'What ploy is this? You have not answered my questions. I demand the satisfaction of an answer.'

John Smith turned, livid, willing the crowd, along with this odious, little man, to disappear into the ether so that he could be alone with her. Instead, intrigued by the appearance of the woman and the promise of polemic, they remained firmly seated, their faces alight with morbid curiosity.

'That's enough. You can all get out now. Yes, all of you. OUT!' He pushed the chair closest to him causing the man on it to slide unceremoniously onto the floor. 'Yes GO, GO,' he raced manically around them, ushering them to the exit, profanities frothing at his mouth like a rabid dog.

'What on earth... John what the hell's going on... Christ...' Griffin, who had just arrived recoiled from the veritable stampede. 'John STOP for Christ's sake, talk to me.' He grabbed John's arm to turn him and pushed him against the gallery wall. 'What the hell do you think you're doing? Have you gone mad?'

'Never mind that.' John Smith's voice softened. 'None of it matters now. Look! It's her.' He turned only to find an empty space where the woman had once stood. 'Christ where is she?'

In a blind panic he raced to the exit of the gallery and down to the great turbine hall searching for her as he went. Had she been an apparition? Was he really going mad? He ran outside and further onto the hostile streets, silently praying for her to reappear, but the streets were quiet now and in the direction he looked only a large, elderly woman trundled by on shapeless, milk bottle legs, fastening him with a timid, plaintive stare that bespoke the loneliness of a loveless existence.

CHAPTER 8

He had awoken, primal and savage like the lord of the flies. She lay in bed, inert and pale while he conducted his orchestra of fear, inside her head, contrasting her passive, slumbering form, her face melancholic, even in repose, to the fearless girl he had once observed galloping across the beach in the gloam on inky steed, oblivious to the rainstorm. She had ridden with high stirrups then, like a jockey, as if anticipating a chequered flag, midnight hair long and flowing as she had dug in her heels and jerked at the bit between the horse's teeth. He had heard her laughter as she'd gripped the saturated reins tightly, the whip's motion a mere caress. He'd been captivated from that moment, had hated the sight of anyone else who provoked that look of tenderness in her. The spirited woman he had worshipped for years had now gone, her eyes betraying her sadness - even their extraordinary colour had faded slightly as if all the melanin had drained from them. At times when she spoke to him, they were like sallow, hueless pools, dry wadies, quenching no man's thirst. Yet he still wanted her, with all the sick desperation of wanting the impossible. He lived for the possibility of her laughter, her affection, to see her former self return to him if only to deride him for the jealousy that crept up on him like the shadow of a pestilent other. If only he could reconjure the beauty of their lives. But as she lay in her remote bed, in a house with a big space in it, in a union of even greater vacuum, she knew he would rather see her dead than relinquish her. He was her nightmare, her incubus.

He had left quietly but did not travel far. He knew she would not be long. And he was right. Anticipating her movements he watched her night face slowly dissolve in the brightness of day, the bleak house left in her wake. For a while she disappeared from sight and he was jealous of that too, of the shadows that remained with her and of the Earth that held her in its gravity. Yet part of him was never gone. She felt him with her, felt his sense of shame, like a second-rate detective left to the sleazy morsels of adultery.

Time passed until the ceaseless rhythm of the sea could no longer be heard. Roads became heavy with impatient traffic and the once walled city appeared like a faded carpet with all its magic wrung out. Historic ghosts from fire and plague played host, vectors of time, now misplaced like many who walked the city pavements, in an alien world. She sensed him withdraw into the shadows like a villain, Bill Sykes without his dog, Jack without his Spot. Dizzy from noise the gallery felt uneasy, the great turbine hall, despite its vast space, as claustrophobic as Poe's black cat. Moving toward the escalator, conscious there was nowhere to hide behind apart from the cold marble of statues, she entered the gallery. He was momentarily forgotten, the condemned man, waiting for judgement day, for her to discover the farce of her existence.

The wait was not long. A few minutes later she reappeared in obvious distress. Tavern eyes drunk with despair she rushed from the gallery onto the streets.

After a while she slowed down and took a different path, a quieter path. She seemed disorientated and stopped for a moment to consider direction. She turned. The only place to hide was a nearby telephone kiosk. Then suddenly an unexpected thing happened. The telephone rang out, shrill against the stillness of the day. She answered it quickly, for fear of the attention it generated. The sound of change connecting another kiosk could be heard, and a woman, sounding slightly breathless.

'Is that you?' she asked. 'Is that you? Don't hang up.'

Too late. She felt the essence of him then, and of danger, of wanting to get out of the kiosk but feeling too conspicuous to leave. She was trapped in the stench, the stench of words and voices, conceived by the rotation of the silver finger dial and propelled through the wire to startle the unsuspecting. The woman at the other end had no doubt expected her lover who was evidently late or else indifferent. Witness box of clandestine lovers. So much news received in that red box. There were fag ends stubbed into the mouthpiece and the slot was jammed with ash and stale whisky piss. Who could forget that stench? Piss and tobacco, life and death, Mr Benson and Mr Hedges the undertakers - customers imprisoned in a vacuum and quite unable to break the glass. Suddenly it was easy to see why that red box had to endure so much abuse. People had no choice. They were trapped, prisoners behind the glass, incarcerated by words in upright coffins. She turned again and pushed, this time more decisively. She must return to the gallery. Whatever she discovered, nothing could be worse than living with this constant fear and uncertainty. And maybe she would uncover the goodness in him. But she felt his scream. She must never leave him. The red iron bars of her prison gave way.

Chapter 9

John Smith stood surveying the dreary London streets listening to the cacophony of sounds, digesting the acrid taste. Too much traffic from the day, both human and motorized had polluted the air creating a haze that obscured the way forward. Perhaps it was true, he thought, that when something or someone spun really fast they disappeared. When they were out of sight they might as well have disappeared. What other explanation could there be?

His agent half turned toward the gallery still conscious of publicity. 'But are you sure it was her? I mean how could it be? You said she was drowned four years ago.'

'It was her.'

'Well of course I'll help in any way I can but...'

'Well, if you really want to help,' John Smith lit a cigarette, 'you'll have to go all the way, like she did. *Help* is simply *hell* without the final P.'

His agent took the cigarette from John Smith and took a deep drag from it. 'I'm afraid it will take my less nimble mind more time to work out any contribution to that statement.'

'Just help me find her will you?' The composure of his voice only vaguely disguised his desperation.

'Of course, but are you *sure* she wasn't a figment of your imagination. I mean, you've been under a lot of pressure lately. Sometimes the mind plays tricks on us. You haven't been drinking?'

'Of course not.'

'Because that could do it. Or even a lack of. I once went without alcohol for three weeks and I swear the lack of hops made me hallucinate.'

'It was her.'

'I saw her too.'

They turned. The small, dark man from the audience faced them squarely. The unwavering truculence with which he had challenged John Smith earlier had gone, replaced by a somewhat laboured composure. 'Yes, I saw your Duchess, or should I say your partner in crime. Very impressive I must say. I was almost fooled myself. Anyway, I saw the direction in which she went.' He added measuredly. 'It looked like she was being followed.'

'Followed?'

'Almost certainly. Perhaps she is in danger? In any case I can describe this man very well but at a price. The price of some answers.'

John Smith lunged at his small, dark shape and thrust him against the wall winding him with the impact. With some effort Griffin pulled him back. 'For Christ's sake man, get a grip. Leave him.' The look of incandescent rage on his friend's face was alien to him. John Smith looked at the man whose demands had cost him those precious moments of concentration and raised his fist but before he could strike a woman's voice interrupted.

'What did you say to my friend?' She glared accusingly at John Smith. 'She'd never have run off like that without good reason, not without me. I told her to wait for me. And you called her Maria. Why did you call her that?'

The men stared at the tall, flustered figure baring her small, white teeth in fleshy gums, the line down the centre of her forehead an ever-deepening chasm.

'And who are you?' the little, dark figure spat, annoyed at the prospect of any further displacement of his time and consideration, despite the fact that her intervention had saved him from harm.

'Who are you?' she retorted.

'Who the hell are you both come to that?' John Smith studied them both warily.

'Look,' Griffin interjected, 'as the one voice of reason here I suggest we all go somewhere and sit down and discuss things sensibly. Squabbling in the street like a bunch of old fish wives won't get us anywhere.'

'No I don't suppose it will.' John Smith glanced contemptuously at the small crowd that was now observing the commotion. 'And I don't suppose it would be very good for publicity either.'

Griffin's apartment was sparsely decorated though devoid of minimalist pedantry. His tastes seemed to Rosy more concordant to an ascetic than an aesthete. The rooms were oddly devoid of art other than a nude sketch in charcoal which hung in the spacious hallway. The walls were bland and the period features seemed anachronistic, juxtaposed with the black leather sofas in which they now sat. Griffin placed steaming mugs on the coffee table. The fact that this was his apartment and his coffee, gave him a sense of governance. He looked, Rosy thought, rather too earnest, like a detective in an inferior murder mystery whose job it was to determine the motives of the suspects. 'I think the first priority,' he said somewhat platitudinously, 'is to establish who we are and our connection to the absent party.' He gestured to Rosy. 'Ladies first.'

'As you wish. My name's Rosy, Rosy Bloom. An attempt at a joke by my parents I imagine. I'm a friend of Catherine's and we came here today in a desperate bid to discover who she is and where she came from, facts elementary to most of us I know, but which seem to have deserted her four or so years ago after a near drowning.'

Rosy relayed her story precisely and succinctly, eager to hear the revelations of others yet unwilling to deny any detail that could prove vital to Catherine's recovery. Throughout she noted John Smith's face, fractured like shattered glass. Griffin poured him a whisky which he downed in one gulp. Its warmth helped stave off the chill of his discovery. His head felt heavy in his hands. He had thought they were in two different worlds, hers silent and his filled only by a relentless, tinnitus scream. Now he realised that the scream had been hers.

'Her instincts were right then?' Rosy took a photograph out of her bag. 'I always carry this with me. I took it last year when we spent a day at the beach. I carry it around with me with the intention of showing it to anyone who I think might know her, which is completely illogical since how would I ever know who might know her?'

John Smith stared at the photograph. 'You know when I first fell in love with her she had a photograph taken for me to remember her by, two in fact, one positioned from the front and one from the side, like those taken for criminal reference. I bought a double frame especially and slid her both into them, *Miss Frontwards* and *Miss Sidewards*.' He was rambling now.

'I'd miscalculated the size of the frame slightly and had to trim the edges of both photographs. Even that hurt horribly. I only wished I'd had a grand piano to place her on. If I could have afforded one I would have bought it specially for the purpose, though of course I can't play.'

Griffin patted his friend on the back in what he felt was an acceptable, masculine gesture of solidarity. 'Well, they say life is stranger than fiction don't they?'

'Do they? Who's they?'

'You know exactly what I'm saying. Don't be facetious.'

'My God, four years. I should have tried harder to find her.'

'You thought she was dead.'

'And all the time she was so near and yet so far, staring at me like a wink on the face of the moon. Poor Maria, how lonely she must have been in her own head. I mean, isn't that the point of memories - to project a warmth and undertones of sanity in an otherwise impersonal and hectic world? To be denied that...to be all alone...I can't imagine.'

'Not quite alone.'

'What do you mean?'

'Not to say that she was happy. She wasn't. That much was clear. We never really talked much about *him*. Any suggestion of him seemed to upset her and we saw her too little to wish that. We've only known her for a year though it seems much longer to all of us, and she's an intensely private person. She preferred talking about him in metaphors, always indirectly. Just before we came she asked how you knew when a marriage was over. She was always talking about having the courage to leave. We had the impression, Anja and I, that she was scared of him. Neither Anja or I ever met him though I once or twice saw someone walking to the farmhouse who I assumed was him. He certainly kept a tight rein on her. She never stayed long, though we never saw any signs that he'd abused her. But you couldn't describe her as a sad person, just a bit quiet at times, a little…' she hesitated, '*otherworldly.*'

The perfect word he thought smiling, wanting her physical presence achingly. He remembered the poem she had been fond of quoting to him about eternity being a great ring of pure and endless light where time beneath it was like a vast shadow in which the world and all her train were hurled. Sometimes at night they'd lay in bed with the curtains drawn back and if they'd seen a moving light they'd joked about it being eternity and, defying Copernicus, direct Earth to follow it past Orion's Belt and Pleiades, making their own constellations. They had invented and reinvented their future together - they'd sometimes written about it in scribbled notes that they found the next day scattered over the floor. And now their future was already their past and she was without him, in a present that rejected all claims to their amphigoric space travel. Oh for the spun warmth of that private world, locking them in an intimacy that had been entirely their own.

'Is this the man you speak of?' The small, dark stranger spoke, passing his camera to Rosy.

'I don't know. Maybe. Of course it's not very clear but he has the same kind of *animalic* - is that a proper word - look about him as the man I saw on the road.'

'You're right. He does appear to be following her.'

John Smith took the camera from her. 'Shit! He could have taken her anywhere. If he's hurt her…'

'You called her Maria. Is that her real name?'

'Yes Maria Cruz.'

'An exotic Spanish name.'

'Yes, though the plan had been to change it to the even more exotic *Smith*.'

'Well, I came here to solve a mystery but I find that you have one of your own to solve obviously much closer to your hearts.' The small, dark stranger reclaimed his camera. 'I thought it was a trick, this woman appearing after all this nonsense about Goya, but I see it was not. Still,' he paused, 'I just might be able to help you.'

'Who *are* you?' Griffin asked the question on everyone's lips.

'My name is Señor Santos Dominguez. If you lived in Spain and worked in the art world you would not have to ask that question. I have studied Goya, and in particular his relationship with the Duchess of Alba for ten years now and I have heard every account possible of their relationship in my search for the truth. Then I heard of this madman in England who claimed to be the reincarnation of Goya. At first I was merely amused but when I saw you being interviewed and the missing painting was spoken of, the one Goya painted of the Duchess of Alba and his child, I began to wonder how you can possibly know what it has taken me so many years to uncover.'

'What do you mean? Are you saying that there really *is* a missing painting and that Goya had a child with the Duchess?' John Smith gestured to Griffin. 'One for the road I think. Señor Dominguez too perhaps?'

Griffin poured them a whisky and took a swig from the bottle. 'Go ahead.'

Señor Dominguez drank his whisky with ease, his expression unchanged by its medicinal warmth. 'There *is* a missing painting of the Duchess with Goya's child though I don't know of its whereabouts. This is a long story and one I have no desire to relay at this moment. I came simply to ask how you came by this information and what you hoped to gain by exploiting it.' His laugh had hollow undertones. 'You have no idea how I have longed for the moment when I can declare in my native land the truth of Goya and Alba's circumstances. But to be believed I would need proof - the painting. Otherwise it remains speculation like all the other claims.'

John Smith laughed, not unkindly. 'Oh dear.' He leaned forward and poured the stranger another whisky. 'My intent was not to deceive *you* sir, a serious scholar. But I have to tell you that this is just an enormous coincidence. My claim is pure fiction, a publicity stunt, courtesy of my agent here Mr Griffin Montague. I'm afraid you have wasted your time and energy on us. We are, as you so aptly declared, impostors.' He laughed again somewhat hysterically this time. 'But you have to see the irony of it and show me some mercy. For you my friend, it is simply a question of reputation and professional integrity. You have lost only a *painting* of a woman and her child, whereas I, I have lost the real thing.' He paused and drew breath as if with some effort. 'You see, Maria was nine months pregnant when I lost her. I suppose the baby died when she nearly drowned.'

'Oh my God, Emily!' Rosy suddenly remembered the little girl. She said, 'This may not seem like a celebratory moment but if I had a cigar I would light it for you. Congratulations John Smith, you have a daughter!'

CHAPTER 10

Belying all descriptions of a heavy heart, grief came to Catherine that following morning in colours. She opened her eyes to a room that had turned smalt blue and she knew immediately that something was badly wrong. Someone needed help. Then she remembered that it was she herself. It was a queer kind of recognition, like staring at a body in a morgue and discovering that it was your own. She despised the blueness of that room because it revealed the truth that sorrow had no obvious or definable face but took whatever form it could. Her head, slumped awkwardly over the side of the bed, hurt, and she raised it with great difficulty. It felt heavy with gloom, like a black rock hanging over the face of the world. She turned and buried it in her pillow silently praying for sleep. For a moment in her dreams she had been free. Now, the small ray of sunlight shining fiercely through the blue haze of the room burned away all deception. She tried to move but her body was racked with pain. She looked down at the sheets which were stained with blood. From this angle, raised on her forearms she could see herself in the dressing room mirror. A handkerchief containing her blood lay on her pillow. Her body was cold and badly bruised. She managed to stand weakly and view her face in the mirror, tracing with the tip of her finger the swollen, blue-purple gradient of impaired flesh which disfigured her face, invaginating almost the eye so that only the minutest glimpse of viridian could be distinguished. She stared at her body in the mirror. She had always thought that the bare facts of nakedness were not intrinsically interesting. Apart from minor distinctions everyone was the same. Quiet, tick, groan, she was universal, the body in the mirror - a nice body as far as she could gauge, though there was nothing to recommend one from another, other than a penchant for more or less of it. Now hers was covered in cuts and bruises, swollen and broken. She felt exposed then, the littered clothes a chimerical testimony to her embarrassment. She would have to pick them up at some point and put them on and in the space of that time accept the circumstances of their removal. The naked and clothed *Maja*. She must have slept for several hours in this blue haze. The curtains wavered slightly in the draught and the room was not quite in focus. The window was much too high to enable her to escape and she was not strong enough in any case. She must be patient, bide her time and try to remember as much as she could from her past. She knew that her liberation would become more palpable with every memory. Then she thought of Emily. If only she could speak to Anja and explain. She wished she had memorised her telephone number but she could not even be sure of her address. She knew though that Anja would take good care of Emily until she returned. She could not remain a prisoner here forever. She could not remain, stolen and violated, sequestered from any hope of escape.

She lay down on the bed and tried to remember. Thoughts of John Smith were a great comfort to her.

She remembered now a time when they had been together, the curtains had been drawn and the stars they had viewed from the window above their bed had seemed to shine with an illusory brightness. Her eyes had fixed upon them and she remembered their games. With those stars they had created new worlds, old worlds, preferred worlds. In the candlelight beneath their vast canopy their own small deceptions were without distinction. These fixed stars and wandering planets had witnessed an eternity of secrets, tacitly and without sententiousness. But somehow they brought her closer to John Smith and she began to remember more clearly. And she knew without question that he was thinking of her now, just as she was him. She remembered being with him by the sea. She had picked up a shell covered with serpulid worm tubes. She remembered him telling her about when he had worked briefly as a fisherman and had almost been drowned far out at sea in a boat riddled with ship worms. Thank God they'd had flares with them he'd said and for a moment, caught up in the image of his beauty, she'd imagined him using his bell-bottomed trousers as sails before she'd realised what he'd meant and laughed. Do you know he'd said, that shells have ears like walls and they contained every secret that was disclosed in their mother of pearl interiors until they were carried away by the tide where they opened up and deposited them on the sea bed for all eternity - the secrets that was. If only people were so loyal. He had turned to her then. 'I couldn't bear it if you ever left me.' She had promised never to leave him and they had wandered further along the beach, impervious to the biting wind that rocked the boats out at sea, still keen to do foolish *lover* things, to pick up rhombic-shaped shells and listen to their stories and to soak each other with frozen salt water. She remembered finding two whelk shells perfectly formed and flawless. They had raced to the waters edge where they had charged their glasses and simulated a toast to the fishermen at sea. And it was then that she had noticed the bottle washed up amongst a cluster of weeds. It had been an old marble stopper bottle in an unusual shade of aqua-green just like the one Emily had found on the beach. The glass had been voluptuous and smooth. He had taken a pen and written her a note before throwing it back into the water. The tide had returned it immediately. *"Where are you? Show me. 'Cry me a river.' Say me a word at the Oracle of Delphi."* How odd that she could remember such an obscure note so readily and yet still struggle to remember her identity.

Yesterday, when she had seen her portrait at the gallery, something in her had been revived. She realised that recognition was more to do with perception than reality. She had never imagined herself this way. Had someone told her that her face would have been excellent if her nose was not so aquiline or that there was something endearing about the irregularity of her smile, that would have been enough. She didn't expect adulation, that was reserved for others - the women you saw on the covers of magazines, smiling their perfect, chalk smiles. But a small acknowledgement would have been nice. Every girl should be told that they are beautiful at least once, even if it was by their mother. At a young age these things were important and little comfort was derived from hearing the general adult consensus about the omnipotence of personality. Even if there had been time to develop one, evidence contradicting its importance was flouted from every medium.

Now of course, she was no longer so very young. The painting had given her a heightened sense of those lost years, of missing words and pictures and reveries that grew from each other, gathering momentum until one was wholly in their rhythm before they suddenly died. These thoughts had occupied her when she had heard John Smith calling her name, not the name she knew as hers but a name that resonated nonetheless. His face had been close to hers then and she was reminded of the previous night, when thoughts of sand and sea and friendship had faded into that vague echo of space just before sleep and his face had been her final image. She recalled his words. 'Maria,' he'd said, 'is that you?'

'Do you know me?' She'd heard herself reply, her voice small and ill-defined. 'Yes, it's me,' she would have preferred to have said. But had it been Ibsen who had said that Man cannot take too much reality? Suddenly reality had frightened her. She'd wanted the truth and then been too afraid to hear it. She'd been vaguely aware of Rosy's arrival and John Smith's angry voice directed at the crowd and the spaces around her growing smaller. She had looked upon the face of 'bold Sir Lancelot,' and now it seemed she must pay the price. She recalled Lord Tennyson's poem.

> She look'd down to Camelot
> Out flew the web and floated wide;
> The mirror crack'd from side to side;
> "The curse is upon me," cried
> The Lady of Shalott.

She had lost herself down the river, her thoughts and limbs deadened, yet even then as she had disappeared she'd known that they had been lovers - soul mates and sinners, not wicked but wilful. She could even recall parts of their conversation. 'We are, we are...' she spoke aloud as if it might hasten the process of recovery, 'no, no, not the Ovaltineys but the *Candle People*.' Yes the ones that lost their heads in the heat of it all. She'd seen a vision of the darkened room, the bed upon which they had lay and the light from the candles. She remembered now, the shadows they had cast had been part of a game. The flame was now out - the last of the molten wax had dripped down those familiar thighs, the kitsch candle thighs of the lovers. She had pressed her fingers into one and was astonished how quickly it had hardened. 'That's because of you,' he had quipped. How perfect it had been. When she had paused for a moment, even in those city streets, she could still recall how her body had weakened in anticipation of his next touch. In essence he was still there, even now, or perhaps a part of him had come away with her. How strange that this should be her first recollection after meeting him.

She had felt ready then to return to the gallery. She had finally been prepared for answers. And Rosy would be worried. She had glanced around her and noticed that she had entered some kind of backwater presumably where no one else wanted to be. She had heard the sound of ringing and it was then that she had noticed the kiosk. Who had been ringing that silent, empty street? Which absent lover had forgotten? One to whom love was no more than a weapon or a perfunctory kindness perhaps. She had felt fear and uncertainty creep back into her bones. London was a vast and lonely city full of emptiness and poverty. Ahead lay the Almshouse and beyond that the rickety bridge with the troll beneath. How to escape that heavily-buttressed poor house and the buffeted faces of strangers in the window; how to fool the troll into thinking she was inedible? Behind her she had heard the telephone kiosk door creaking. Fear of *him* returning to claim her froze her suddenly.

'Don't be afraid,' she had heard him say, 'I love you.'

She had almost felt then his hands traverse her face and body, drawing out its details, almost smelt the faint, natural odour of his palms as they had enclosed her nostrils, and the taste of the sea as his fingers probed for her absent words.

'What do you know about love,' she had thought. 'I could tell you better what love isn't. It isn't, for example, having a ring put through my nose, or my being controlled or attached.'

Chapter 11

John Smith awoke in the stupefied haze of his new reality. It was odd, he thought, that what in other circumstances would have been a very ordinary revelation, had so radically altered the dynamics of his existence. He was a father, a fact that had been concealed from him for four years, undetected by premonition or instinct, left only to the happy indiscretions of Lady Serendipity, or even more frighteningly, the mischievous whisperings of those fickle astral goblins. He may never have known, may have gone through his entire life with his head in a trough. It was this thought above all, that left him petrified, his features temporarily turned to granite like a face carved into Stone Mountain.

Rosy placed a coffee cup next to him. She smiled. 'God you look rough. I suppose you're still getting over the shock of yesterday.'

'Well,' he sat up with some effort, his left side aching from the discomfort of the sofa. 'I can't say yesterday was a flat day,' he rubbed his aching shoulder ruefully, 'but then neither was it round or conical, and it certainly wasn't comical.'

'Finding out that you're a father must have come as something of a surprise?'

'Yes, the best surprise of my life.' He held the dark liquid to his lips and drank in its warmth. 'It's all a bit overwhelming to tell the truth. I can't quite get my head around it. I keep imagining my daughter, her defiant and somewhat premature entrance into this muddled world, pink, cone-headed, uncooked and already I want to disembowel anybody who finds her less than perfect. One of the most important moments in my life and I missed it. And as we speak I'm missing everything about her as she dances her way all too quickly into burgeoning womanhood. I want a hand in influencing her thoughts, her actions, her morality. Now that's a word I haven't used in a long time. It's crazy, I mean...' he looked at Rosy with a look of disbelief, 'how can I feel such utter devotion for someone I haven't even met? She's not mine, not in the truest sense. We own nothing in life, especially not our children and they owe us nothing. All conceptions are the result of fornication after all. It's not exactly an onerous task. Our job is just that of custodians to our land, our possessions, our offspring. It's funny though, despite her frailty and tender years I feel more vulnerable than she. All she has to do to be worshipped, cosseted and adored by me is to exist, whereas God knows how I will win her affection. I don't know anything about children.'

'Just be yourself. That's all you can do. Children recognise when they are loved. That's all they need.'

'And what can I possibly tell her about her mother?'

'We'll find her.' Rosy spoke with a confidence she no longer felt.

Griffin entered the room looking clean-shaven, his hair neatly combed, gelled and sprayed into motionlessness.

'Christ, what is that stuff you put on your head? Don't you worry about the ozone layers?'

'I see being told you're a father's done nothing to improve your manners. You look like crap by the way.'

'Hardly surprising. I feel like a badger torn from its set. How come I got the sofa and not Señor Santos Dominguez?'

'You were the last to bed. Remember? You were out most of the night looking for Maria.'

'Maria,' Rosy mused, 'I still can't get used to calling her that.'

John Smith sighed. 'I don't remember much about last night. I remember the clock striking one. Perhaps a doleful reminder that the good times are over. Down I fell...hickory, dickory Dixon dock.' He pulled on his shoes. 'This is the first time I can remember wearing the same underwear for more than one day. When I pulled on my socks just now I felt something give, several things in fact, like my whole persona and the meaning of life.' He finished the last of his coffee. 'I think there must have been a structural weakness somewhere above the heel. A little hole has formed there and one seems to be appearing in the other sock too in the same region. Perhaps from the strain of two days in my shoes. Everything seems so confused.' He sighed in exasperation. 'I feel I must go home and feed my underwear and change the hamster. I'm a father. I still can't believe it. All these wasted years. Maria must have been through hell.'

'It wasn't your fault. You couldn't possibly have known.'

Señor Dominguez entered the room. Rosy liked his slightness. Despite his small stature there was, she thought, a despotic air about him that she was drawn to.

'Coffee?'

'Thank you yes. With some toast perhaps?'

Ordinarily this would have irritated Rosy but she was pleased for an excuse to feign subservience. The truth was she wanted to feel useful. Since Catherine had disappeared she had felt a tremendous burden of guilt. It was she, after all, who had devised the plan to come to London. She knew how vulnerable Catherine had been. She should have watched her more stringently. She made toast, mounds of it and took it to the table with butter and fresh coffee.

'Are we expecting an army?'

'It's my fault,' she sat mopishly. 'I was responsible for her. Anja would never have left her. She would have been more careful.'

John Smith reached across and touched her hand. 'No,' he said, 'you've done nothing wrong. You've just been a friend to her. If anyone is to blame it's me for losing her all those years ago. She wanted me to go with her that night on the boat you know, but I was too busy. I wanted to finish some painting or other.' He sighed and released her hand. 'Even now I sit up in bed watching the night turn to day, searching for some means of ameliorating the guilt - trying to weave some humour into the tangled web. It's not easy. One smile a night is above average.'

Griffin began his second round of toast. 'Surely,' he said, 'it's now a police matter.'

'Perhaps you're right,' John's face, slightly distorted in the morning light seemed suddenly anguished. 'She is after all, registered as dead. When the authorities are alerted to the circumstances they'll surely stop at nothing to find her.'

Señor Dominguez laughed, not unkindly. 'My friends, this is a vast city is it not? How many missing persons do you think it has seen? And your story?' He shrugged. 'A woman who was drowned four years ago has become resurrected! Are you absolutely sure that the woman you saw is her? Could it not be wishful thinking? How much have you wanted her since that night? Too much perhaps?'

'It was her.'

'It's not me that doubts you my friend. But I think that you need to think this out very carefully before you take any action that may, let us say, compromise her.'

'Compromise her?'

'She has a husband does she not? Or at least someone who claims to be. And that type of husband, I would surmise, is the dangerous kind. I expect he would stop at nothing to keep her from her past life.'

'What are you saying?'

'Only this.' He picked up the digital camera once more. 'I have been examining the photographs I took and look at the way he stalks her.' He passed the camera to John Smith. 'Does he not seem determined? Look again at the next photograph. The distance between them is closer is it not? He is not wasting any time. He has already the look of a hunted animal. And it is never good to corner such an animal.'

'You sound like a Spanish version of Poirot.'

'Let me see.' Rosy took the camera. The man in question was difficult to see clearly. The first image showed him from behind and the second from the side with his face turned away, but she recognised something about his stance, the lofty conceitedness of his vaguely bestial form. 'That must be him,' she said, 'that must be her husband. My God!' She understood now. 'He must have followed us here.'

Anger consumed John Smith, and along with anger the inevitable, painful throb of certainty of his own part in events. It occasioned him no relief that she had apparently been loved. Unrequited love was a useless and dangerous condition. In deference to Rosy he modified his thoughts and simply said, 'We need to find her as quickly as we can.'

'Indeed you do my friend,' Santos continued eating toast, 'without the police I think. We don't want to make him panic so that he acts irrationally.'

'Irrationally! You're talking about a man who kidnaps a woman with amnesia and claims to be her husband. Hardly the act of a rational man to begin with.'

'Exactly, which is why you should do nothing more to alarm him.' He turned to Rosy. 'I suggest you look in the obvious places first.'

'What obvious places?' Rosy was impressed by his assertiveness. 'I can't think of anywhere obvious.'

'Where is home?'

'Cornwall.'

'Then I suspect he has gone there with her. After all where else can he go? He needs time to think of a plan. Until yesterday he presumably had no idea that any of this was going to happen. And he will not realize that he has been photographed. He will assume anyone looking for her will be looking in London.'

'Brilliant.' Rosy was impressed. 'We should get on the trail right away, before it goes cold.'

'And if you're wrong?' Griffin wasn't too keen on having his suggestions quashed. 'The police may have better methods of finding her.'

'She is not of an age that would concern the police too much. She has only been missing for a night. A grown woman away from home for the night does not seem so much cause for alarm.'

'He's right,' John conceded. 'They would probably laugh at us.'

'In that case,' Griffin, determined to contribute something of worth, but also thinking laterally, smiled broadly, 'one of us should stay at the gallery in case she returns. Since I'm responsible for the exhibition I suggest that this should be me. And you others, well, you should go to Cornwall as Señor Santos er Dom… suggests.'

'Dominguez, but please call me Santos.'

'Well it does make sense.' Rosy was eager to take some action. 'But will you be coming with us Santos? I mean now that you've discovered the truth about Goya here I see no reason for you to concern yourself with our plight. I expect you'll want to return to Spain at the earliest opportunity.'

'On the contrary. You have all captivated me in some way. It is an intriguing situation. I would like to know that the lady in question is found and harmony restored and I also believe that I may be able to use this in some way in my writing so my offer of help is not entirely altruistic. Also my intrigue with our Goya here is not quite over.' He nodded toward John. 'Nothing, in fact could persuade me to retreat at such a time.' He smiled his lop-sided smile. 'That is of course, if you will allow?'

'Of course.' She looked at John Smith who for once was contrite.

'We need all the help we can get my friend and if you want an interview with Goya for some Spanish magazine then I probably owe you that much.'

'Let us just hope that our Duchess is found without delay.'

'Yes,' John sighed, 'it's one of those moments when I silently pray though I'm not a believer. A part of my heritage I suppose. A remnant of those Sundays long ago with my mother dragging me to that perennially frozen Sunday church, her long-suffering eyes clamped solemnly in prayer.' He remembered the collections yielded in ancient tradition by wooden boxes fastened to long sticks that stretched down the pews when everyone had tried to put in the least amount possible without being observed by their neighbours. His mother had always sat with him in the gallery of which there had been three - "*one, two, three, mother caught a flea.*" He had always been allowed to choose which one but once seated had always been dissatisfied. The minister in the pulpit had been the only person who had been able to see all parts of the church and he had envied him that distraction. Still, his own prayers had at least been answered when the sermon had ended. His mother's on the other hand were forever dispelled by the sight of his father scraping his hectoring boots on the grating and cursing for his Sunday dinner. 'Tell me,' he searched Rosy's face for the truth, 'did he treat her very badly?' He couldn't bear to think of Maria suffering as his own mother had while he'd remained in unwitting ignorance.

'Well he never hit her if that's what you mean. We would have seen the evidence. I imagine he was just controlling, though she never really spoke of him to be truthful. She's such a private person that any enquiries seemed like an invasion of her privacy. It's more what we surmised from what she didn't say. And maybe that's a dangerous way to know a person. He kept her as isolated as he could that's for sure. But of course now we can understand why.'

'Are you sure? Are you sure that he won't hurt her?'

'That is perhaps an unfair question.' Señor Dominguez hesitated, not wishing to alarm, but then continued. 'He is now a little desperate after all. I think we must expect the unexpected.'

'If he touches her... If he harms one hair on her head...'

'You need to start thinking with yours before he does.'

'What do you mean?'

Señor Dominguez smiled. 'You need to start thinking like your alter ego my friend - like the great Francisco de Goya.'

'I never want to think of Goya again. I'm tired of that whole charade.'

'Not so fast,' his slight figure belied, Rosy felt, his air of command, 'without your pretence of Goya you may never have rediscovered her.'

John Smith had to admit that this was true.

'Then think again my friend and be assured that Goya would have kept his head and would certainly not have allowed himself to be outwitted by this imbecile.'

Rosy laughed. 'You're as bad as he is. How can you possibly know what Goya would or would not have done? All you can do is surmise, just like Anja and I.'

'Not true. You see, I have been a student of Goya for many, many years now and I feel I know exactly how he would react. You see,' he leaned a little closer to Rosy, 'Goya was a very clever man. He had to be. He survived and flourished in turbulent times. He understood how, not only the system but his fellow man worked and he played this to his advantage with a foot in both camps.'

'Which camps?' Rosy looked confused.

'Oh my dear,' Senior Dominguez stood as if for effect, 'I will try not to bore you with too much detail but you see, Goya was born in Aragon at a time when Spain was regionally compartmentalized so considered himself more Aragonese than Spanish. He also lived close to the French border and was essentially an *afrancesado*, a Francophile, so his sense of national identity was complicated by these factors. Intellectually he considered himself an *ilustrado*, a sympathiser of the Enlightenment, a character who embraced social progress and modernisation. The *pueblo* or the Spanish working classes for whom Goya had a great affection, were generally hostile to the *ilustrados*, whose reforms were not profitable to them. As they saw it, the Enlightenment was a threat to their traditional, conservative way of life. Goya's loyalties between *pueblo* and *ilustrado* were further confused by his parents, one of whom was a minor aristocrat and the other who was a craftsperson.'

'Your point being?'

'Simply that whatever sympathies Goya felt for the *pueblo* and toward the Enlightenment his appointment since 1786 was that of Painter to the King. His livelihood therefore depended on pleasing the monarchy and that is the political decision that he made to save himself from possible starvation. Yet within the confines of his work he stayed faithful to his ideals. His blatant social and political commentary in the *Caprichos* series, which ridiculed greed, superstition and other unenlightened aspects of Spanish society, undermined the establishment and this was not lost on the Spanish Inquisition who at one point ordered the withdrawal of all copies. Of course toward the end of his life, Goya fled to France where many of his friends had lived in exile for many years.' He sighed. 'The point I am making is that Goya managed to manipulate any situation to his advantage. He was a man of great charm who, despite his admiration for the fairer sex, managed to think with his head and not his heart and this is what *you* have to do my friend. There is no occasion for error. Yes of course you are in shock. You have not only just rediscovered your great love but also learned that you have a daughter. That is enough to make any man act foolishly. But you must be calm and think, what would the great Francisco de Goya do in your situation? How would he have saved his Duchess of Alba? On these thoughts alone you must concentrate.'

'Santos is right.' Rosy stood, inspired. 'But we should go now. Griffin, will oversee the exhibition and, of course, contact us immediately if he sees Maria.'

'Naturally,' Griffin smiled at John, sympathetic, but eager now to return to the gallery. 'You can be assured, that I'll be especially vigilant.'

Rosy turned to John and Santos Dominguez. 'We should make tracks. Anja will be keen to know what progress has been made, and of course,' she met John's eyes which were filled with a remote terror, 'you'll be keen to meet your daughter.'

CHAPTER 12

Anja watched her children playing as she hung out the washing, *the young bairns of her past desire*, as Rosy had once jokingly referred to them. It was odd but she could barely remember a time when her belly was flat and her nipples weren't stretched like corks from too many suckling babies. Once you had children it was as if, she thought, your own life was substantiated only through theirs. Without them you were incomplete, like half a person needing their presence to make you whole again. She wondered how Catherine was coping without Emily. The little girl was laughing now as she was chased around the silver birch they all called the lightening tree, struck as it had been in only its fourth year of growth, but earlier that morning it had been difficult to console her. She and her mother had never before been parted.

Hilda sat nearby on the doorstep, eyes oblivious, staring into the distance. 'A *pfennig* for them Hilda.' But Hilda was somewhere else, trapped within her wall of thoughts. Anja pulled back her lank hair. There was a kind of lost prettiness about her that revealed itself from time to time in her worried smile as she watched, the children, her mother-in-law, the space where she had last seen Catherine and Rosy. It had only been yesterday but it seemed long ago when Catherine had said goodbye, her dark hair outlined sharply against the brightness of the day, smiling in anticipation of what she might discover. Anja had smiled back and wished her luck but something inside her, something intuitive and inexplicable, had recoiled at her departure. Now she was missing and Anja could only try to busy herself while she awaited news, take care of the children, the old woman, her house. Her art must wait. She could not paint with these feelings of angst gnawing at her. If only she could do something more productive. But no, her job was to wait and watch, that sorry, impotent role for which women of her kind were so used. She suddenly feared for Emily. What if *he* came to take her? How would she manage with just a few children and an old woman as defence? From what Rosy had said on the telephone he was capable of anything. For once, despite their battles she wished her husband was there but he was working away for two weeks on the east coast, or so he had said. She wished her late mother was there to advise her. "Why me?" Anja had used to ask snivelling into her mother's old favourite paisley scarf.

"*Warum ist der Himmel blau?*" Why is the sky blue? Her mother would answer in the same way to everything she didn't understand, which was quite a lot. And how did the world begin? And what came first, the chicken or the egg? (Razor-thin shoulders urged through satin blouse, crumpled face searching reluctantly for truths). "It is not for us to question."

Hilda called suddenly from the steps needing assistance. Despite her slight frame the awkwardness of her balance made her difficult to lift.

'It's a man I need really.'

'At your age Hilda?'

'It's hard to get up.'

'*Ja,* I see.' From this vista Anja could view the distant sea and hear its endless rhythm. 'It must be hard without the leg I'm sure.'

'Only when I want to dance.'

Anja smiled. 'I expect you did a lot of dancing Hilda, when you were young.'

The old woman's face brightened with recollection. 'We used to have someone come to play at the church hall but all the organist could play was *Wheels,* again and again, over and over. It's hard to dance to *Wheels.*'

'I can imagine.'

Hilda broke into a tuneless version of the song.

'Quite the songbird aren't you. How about, *Roll out the Barrels...*'

'No.'

'I know, *I Dream of Jeanie with the Light Brown Hair.*'

'I don't want to sing anymore.'

'No?'

'No. All that singing's reminded me of Twinkletoes. He used to sing. I wish I could remember what I did with him. Can't remember a thing.'

'You said you wrapped him in a newspaper. Maybe you buried him in the garden somewhere?'

'Hmmm,' Hilda paused, 'sometimes I think I've got that disease, that Old Heimer thing.'

'*Alzheimer's* Disease.' Anja helped the old lady to the nearest armchair. 'It's a German word, difficult to remember.'

'German is it? I suppose you Krauts must've been the first to suffer from it. Like German Measles.' She paused thoughtfully. 'Whatever they say about you Krauts you've been unlucky like that.'

Anja laughed. '*Ja,* you are right. But never mind, I will put the kettle on and make a cup of very English tea to serve with some very English Victorian Sponge *kuchen.*'

'I'd rather have a coconut mushroom. Pal George always used to have a bag in his pocket. I saw him the other day.'

'You can't have Hilda. He died many years ago.'

'No, not him. Bill Shed. He was being pushed through the town in a wheelchair. Now *he* used to keep birds.'

Anja felt a strange comfort in the old woman's inane ramblings, as though the world that she inhabited, and from which she viewed her insular and modified version of events would disallow any possibility of injuriousness. She felt safe in this world. She could handle the ailing and the idiosyncratic - what she could not tolerate was the sensation she now had of being watched, as if her life, as prosaic as it was, was now under scrutiny, each small and insignificant detail of it. Somewhere out there this crazy man had Catherine. And Catherine, she knew, would not function well without her daughter. She felt sure that he would come for Emily. She had to keep her safe or they may lose Catherine forever. Soon Rosy would return and with her she would bring John Smith and Señor Santos Dominguez and maybe they would bring fresh news. She couldn't help but feel excitement at the thought of meeting these new acquaintances. She seldom got the opportunity to talk about art with anyone other than her closest friends and, had circumstances been different the prospect of sharing an evening over a glass of wine, would have pleased her greatly.

Although it was still relatively early she called the children inside and, despite their protests this time she did not acquiesce. She locked the door behind them and enlisted their help in producing vast amounts of spaghetti and sauce. 'We're expecting visitors soon. Rosy and a couple of men, an artist and an art historian are coming to say hello so make sure you have made enough food.'

'What's an art historian?'

'Someone who knows a great deal about the history of art.'

'Art doesn't have a history.'

'It does if you painted it a long time ago.'

'Like in a cave.'

'*Ja*, exactly.'

'There are some in Lascaux in France.' Her eldest son Rudy never ceased to amaze her. Most of the time he seemed to absorb nothing due to his intense boredom with life but then he would occasion her with particles of information that proved that he actually belonged to the living world.

'Very good. And where did you hear about the caves.'

'Dunno.'

Anja smiled. She knew that he was irritated that he had allowed himself to be caught out.

'Is he a caveman, this man that's coming.'

'No Ilse, not a caveman.'

'Stupid,' Rudy contributed.

'No I'm not.'

'No of course you are not.'

'Is mummy coming home too?' Emily added.

'Not tonight *kinderlein*. But soon, very soon I hope.'

'P'raps he wasn't dead after all,' Hilda interjected, gazing out of the window. 'P'raps he just flew away.'

'What Hilda?'

'P'raps he just flew away.'

Anja looked in the direction of Hilda's gaze. Another rainbow. The light playing tricks again. She had a mistrust of rainbows. There had been a rainbow on the day of her wedding. Her mother had always said it was a bad omen, that whenever a rainbow appeared some poor soul was about to meet their maker, to tread the rainbow bridge to heaven or hell, or in Anja's case - nuptial perdition. 'It'll be coming for me soon,' she'd said, shortly before she'd died so that whenever Anja saw a rainbow thereafter, it had conjured up images of her mother. Sometimes she'd felt she could almost see her waving down, not frantically, but wearing a crowning smile of great joy, safe in the knowledge that it was now *she* who was tricking the *light*. When she'd died, Anja, in tribute and in memory of her mother, had purchased a tree which she'd planted as a living memorial to her. The tree, she'd liked to think, would provide fresh air and cool respite for all who passed by it in years to come. Sadly it had been struck in its fourth year and the only sign of life it now showed in Spring was from the parasitical clematis that weaved and clung to its blackened boughs. Right now it appeared to have a menacing quality. She tugged sharply at the orange curtains. 'We shall look for him in the morning Hilda. *Na, Ja*, all will be well in the morning.'

Chapter 13

Rosy found the enforced proximity of Santos Dominguez more than favourable. She sat in the passenger seat of the old, borrowed and blue BMW, generously offered by Griffin after her own transportation had coughed and spluttered painfully into reluctant motion. John Smith drove and Santos Dominguez in the back amongst the luggage, leaned forward, his hand carelessly brushing against her shoulder, his breath warm against the nape of her neck as he spoke of Goya and the Duchess of Alba.

'What I don't understand,' she said, 'is quite why you would take John's claims seriously enough to travel from Spain to meet him. Why didn't you just dismiss him as another English eccentric or crazy artist?'

'Yes, I will come to this. Of course his art is a work of genius, exceptional, so comparable to Goya's in its execution that even experts may be fooled.'

'Thank you. Praise indeed from such an *aficionado*.'

'But of course alone that would not have been enough. I wanted to know if he was mad or simply deluded. Many people believe that an artistic sensibility predisposes one to mental instability, or even that art itself is a form of madness - a socially acceptable way in which psychotic and neurotic behaviour can be expressed. The most powerful advocate of the art-as-illness theory being, of course, Freud himself.'

John momentarily detached his hands from the driving wheel. 'Something no doubt to do with an unsatisfactory negotiation of the traumas of infancy.'

'Correct my friend,' Santos continued, 'he believed that art was a *substitute gratification*, an illusion rather than reality.'

'I don't understand that idea.' Rosy settled back into her seat. She liked the way Santos's eyes became animated in explanation. It was curious how seductive enthusiasm could be, even if you weren't particularly interested in elucidation.

'Well, yes it is a difficult concept, but in layman's terms, it simply means that instead of a person showing obvious signs of neurosis, their activities are sublimated in the guise of artistic creativity.' He paused. 'Now take our new friend here. He suffered a great loss several years ago which was never really satisfactorily dealt with. But his art, in contrast, has flourished.'

'But he's not mad, just an impostor.'

John raised his hands again from the wheel in mock irritation. 'Yes, the lesser of two evils wouldn't you agree?'

'Who is to say my dear Rosy, that he is not *also* mad?'

John Smith cast a disapproving glance at Santos Dominguez in the mirror. 'I suppose there's a certain advantage to being spoken about in the third person. It allows you to view yourself from a fresh perspective. However, the concern is you might not like what you hear and it sure as hell doesn't feel very inclusive.'

Santos Dominguez continued undeterred. 'The term *madness* lacks technical specificity and so, is notoriously difficult to define. It can stand for every variety of psychological disorders from eccentricity to psychosis and for any set of notions or actions that are unacceptable in terms of traditional social norms. It is *not*, I think you will both agree, *normal* to pretend that you are someone who you are not.'

'Nothing more than an elaborate and lucrative joke, I can assure you. One which would cause amusement in the art world and contention outside it. The brainchild of my agent who has a keener business sense than I. But then you already know that.'

'All the same, only *you* could carry off such a deception. Only you. *Solo Goya*. Was there not, in all honesty, a part of you that believed, if only for a moment, that you might really be the reincarnation of Francisco de Goya?'

'Never, that would be ridiculous.'

'*Never* is a definitive word my friend. I do not believe in absolutes. Think carefully before you say never. Why, for example, did you choose to recreate the Duchess in Maria's image? There are similarities between these women, yes. They are both exceptionally beautiful. Both are dark haired with pale skin, both are slender and perfectly proportioned. But do they look alike? I would argue that they do not. That is the illusion that you have created for yourself, and you have done it brilliantly. We are all now living your fantasy.'

'That's preposterous.' For some reason he could not fathom, John Smith had begun to feel uncomfortable. He had a reluctant admiration for Santos Dominguez. Santos had a keen mind and a dogged determination about him that made John feel, at times, exposed, like a fish in a gill net caught between freedom and captivity, animation and lack of it. It was true that there were times he had doubted his own ability to reason where Maria was concerned but never his own sanity. 'Preposterous,' he repeated, 'that would support your theory that I'm a complete crackpot, which, oddly enough, I am keen to refute.'

'You should not worry my friend. Those who lose the ability to reason through trauma are usually only irrational for limited periods of time. In your case I am not suggesting that you have a *dementing* illness.'

'Well, thank God for small mercies.'

'No, if you have suffered bouts of madness then they are not permanent, just a temporary expression of your loss and an overwhelming desire to regain what you once had.'

'You're saying I'm a basket case.'

Santos sighed in irritation. 'You are deliberately missing my point. Come now, you are an extremely intelligent man, an eloquent man, a man of exceptional talent and good looks too. You would, I imagine, have great appeal for the ladies. How many women have you slept with since you lost Maria?'

'None of your business!'

'Too many perhaps?'

'Perhaps.' He thought, with an aching, ignominious sadness of his own rutting form, spent, not from love, but an endless desperation. Lust was so much easier, so unexacting in time and expectations, though less satisfactory in conclusion. It still left his heart untouched, his haunted, aching need for her resolute.

'And have any of these lovers ever come close to what you felt for *her*?'

'Never.'

'I thought not. So for the last four or so years you have grieved, tormenting yourself with her image, the fact that you could not save her. And as your soul deteriorates your art improves.'

'That's a matter of opinion.'

'I have seen your previous work. It is very good but not exceptional in the way you now paint. Have you ever considered that your trauma has been a necessary catalyst for your present abilities?'

'Nonsense. It's just the way my work has evolved. We learn, we improve and refine - it's called experience.'

Santos Dominguez seemed oblivious to John Smith's protests. 'It may also be that suffering extreme trauma, just as in taking substances, can add another dimension to your work. Think of Van Gogh, Rousseau, Balzak, Blake, Ruskin, Pollock, not forgetting the great Goya himself. They have all been accused of madness at some point. Unfortunately the genius, it appears, is destined to suffer. It seems sadly ironic that his or her pain is to the advantage of the rest of us mere mortals.'

'Well,' John smiled a crusty, sardonic smile, 'put like that I suppose I should be grateful that I'm living in the present age. Otherwise, I would no doubt be in Bedlam, chained to a post, providing entertainment for the voyeuristic masses including yourselves.'

'Oh, I suspect we would be with you my friend. I had a wife once. It is because of my obsession with Goya and Alba that she left. I had so little time for her. Imagine, a beautiful woman at home and I preferred my office and my research. Is that not a sure sign of madness?' He laughed heartily. 'You are not alone.'

John Smith glanced at the speedometer and lessened acceleration. 'I believe the dramatist Nathaniel Lee spent some years at Bedlam. He's known to have said of the authorities that put him there, "*They called me mad,*

I called them mad and damn it, they outvoted me." Now that's what I call a sense of humour.'

'Most of us would have been there at some point. Even, I suspect, our charming companion.'

'Don't bring me into this.' Rosy smiled good-naturedly. 'I'm sane to the point of boring. Anyway,' she was keen to discover more about Santos Dominguez, 'that still doesn't explain why you took the trouble to come to England.'

'Patience I am coming to this.' He spoke in a quieter voice now and his eyes, initially wary, seemed to make a decision to continue. 'What I am about to tell you is still classified information but I will trust you both. In the short time we have known each other I have grown to like you both. Recently I made a great breakthrough in my research. How I came by this location I cannot say but I discovered some letters found in a secret compartment at the *Palacio de Medina Sidonia* at Sanlucar de Barrameda. Goya of course, visited Alba there many times. It is where their affair began. These correspondences, if genuine, leave us in no doubt of their love affair. In two of them, written by Goya to a friend shortly after Alba's death, he speaks of painting her with their child in an effort to immortalise her. Shortly after this the painting was stolen.'

'They really had a child together? That's incredible. I assumed earlier that it was pure undocumented speculation.'

'What happened to the baby?' Rosy interjected.

'She was brought up by a friend of Alba's. Goya visited her regularly.'

'And do you believe that these letters are genuine?'

'I was at the point of authenticating them when I heard of John Smith and his allegations. Can you imagine? I am on the verge of the most magnificent breakthrough, with facts that would astonish the art world. Alba had indeed had a child, a little girl, and had died in childbirth. Goya painted them together from memory just as you did with Maria, but the painting remained hidden for fear of scandal. And suddenly after all these years of study, our friend here is not only making similar claims, but also professing that he is the reincarnation of the great Goya and that he actually fathered this child. I believe you English have a phrase about stealing someone's thunder. Can you imagine how I felt? My first thought was, how could he possibly know these details concerning the Duchess and her child and the missing painting? Of course the affair was covered up at the time. It would have proved too scandalous you see. It would have shown beyond any doubt that they began their affair only weeks after the death of Alba's husband Don José María Álvarez de Toledo y Gonzaga, 15th Duke of Medina Sidonia. And though it was not unusual or even frowned upon necessarily for a woman to have a *cortejos*, a lover, Alba was a patron of Goya - he was not her equal. And after such an obscenely short amount of time after her husband's death, she would undoubtedly have been vilified. When he painted *Black Duchess*, she was still supposed to be in mourning - yet she wears his ring, points to his name...*Solo Goya*. Goya was also married of course to Josefa Bayeu and there was the additional complication of the Spanish Inquisition. They had interrogated Goya several times concerning his politics. It is no secret they believed him a heretic. Toward the end of his life he was forced into exile in France with Leocadia Weiss, his companion since the death of his wife. Goya painted her as the *Black*

Duchess, almost as if he was trying to recreate Alba. Anyway, the *Caprichos* series were etchings containing much social satire. As I said, many of them would be interpreted as ridiculing the church and the Inquisition. Goya had to withdraw them. These were dangerous times for a free thinker like Goya.'

John Smith pulled into a lay-by and stopped the car. He turned to Santos Dominguez with a look of incredulity. 'Let's get this straight. You're saying that Goya really fathered a daughter with Alba? I mean, this is unbelievable, an incredible coincidence. Are you sure that you haven't read something into these letters that doesn't exist? Something you wanted to hear perhaps after hearing of my entirely fraudulent claims?'

'I am quite sure. The painting of Alba and their child is mentioned in the letters several times. Alba was very fond of children but believed she couldn't have any. That's why she adopted María de la Luz, the little black girl. There is an ink wash of Alba holding Maria around 1796. Her expression is of great tenderness. She could not bear the idea of a life without children. Oh yes, adopting from different creeds and cultures is not a modern phenomenon of the rich and famous.' He sighed. 'Sometimes it seems that everything begins and ends with Goya. And as for Alba…when he gave her this gift, her love for him was complete, but only as it happened, destined to be short-lived. She died in labour or, more accurately within a couple of hours of labour. It is said that, either her life, or that of the baby could be spared, and that the Duchess made the decision. She chose life for her child and made the ultimate sacrifice.' Santos

Dominguez spoke quietly and with obvious reverence. 'Much is spoken of Alba's beauty, her wit, her charms, but she was also brave beyond measure. And she made sure that all those close to her were taken care of financially and otherwise. Despite the great suffering of her final hours her concern was for her loved ones. She was a magnificent woman. It is no wonder that Goya adored her. Of course,' he added as though it was indisputable, 'he never recovered from her death. His mental instability was exacerbated by the trauma and his physical health worsened also. His wife was said to have hated the Duchess even more in death than in life. While she was alive she was human at least, with all that that implies, but in death she was deified.'

'What a tragic story.' Rosy thought suddenly of Catherine. 'How alone the Duchess must have felt.'

'Goya was with her to the end. They lay together in their special secret room at the palace which allowed for a view of the stars. They used to lie in the candlelit darkness and speak together of their dreams, of their plans for a life together. In that room she gave birth and in that bed, beneath the stars, she spent her last hours in Goya's arms.'

'Beneath the stars,' John Smith began, but ended quickly, 'I suppose that kind of scenario is typical for many lovers - candlelight, stars, discussions of the future. Nothing very original there.' But he was momentarily lost in that old, private world where he, like Goya, had lay stargazing in the arms of the woman he loved, the molten cortex of the burning candles lapping in their ears along with the heat of sex. He saw a defeated Goya too, oppressed, demoralised, despairing in his conical-hatted isolation, interrogated by the Spanish

Inquisition, endless identical lines of them, their accusatory faces twisted manically in cut-throat fanaticism. What did it all mean? Was he really losing his mind? He had almost lost his mind with jealousy when Maria had lived. Jealousy was surely a form of madness. But that was not something he cared to remember. Where was she? He sighed. Somewhere between the earthbound shadows and the distant Super Novas the astral goblins were no doubt giggling and dancing on all the answers.

CHAPTER 14

Whether it was due to the injuries she had received she couldn't say, but lying in that unfamiliar bed in her quiet pain memories began to return with a new and significant clarity. The layers of oblivion began to unravel as if by some queer, gradual process of exfoliation. For the first time in four years she remembered her parents and it was with a great sense of disappointment that she recollected her mother's image, skeletal and severe, her face like a dried raisin. Her father's image came simultaneously, lean and weak of chin. She remembered then his bigoted, somewhat draconian nature and with it the mock Tudor house in London's suburbs in which they had all lived. All the houses in the neighbourhood had been the same she remembered, imitating one thing or another, designed she supposed for that particular brand of the middle-classes who aspired to buy the original but couldn't quite afford it. She had disliked the pretentiousness of it that extended to her parents, affecting the way they had viewed the world. She had liked to blame the house for this because it offered hope that, were they to be detached from it, reinstated in their former pre-war semi, they might have regained some of the warmth that emanated from her earliest childhood recollections.

She remembered she had returned from her studies at regular intervals. Her parents had exhibited little pleasure in her return yet had wanted her there all the same as she was part of their dissemblance, the devoted daughter returning briefly to the fold for parental instruction. She could visualise their faces now, stern and officious, her mother's in particular detached from all that was real or meaningful, their concern was with image and status, their chief pride the possessions that they had acquired. "It's Clarice Cliff of course," her mother would say, referring to the art deco tea set, a recent acquisition. "Of course many people find her designs a little gaudy but we find them charming, don't we dear?" *Charming* was the word she used to describe anything for which she had no technical description. At least she lacked esoteric purpose, unlike her father whose desire for elitism meant that his meaning was often buried beneath his language, not illuminated by it. But they were not her biological parents. She was their adoptive child. She remembered them disclosing this information when she was about fifteen. Her parents, they said, had died in a tragic accident. They had expected tears but she had accepted the situation without qualms and a part of her had been relieved. She was not like them. It was not in her blood to be like them. She had been glad. Strange that she should remember nothing of her parents for so long and then these small, unhappy details. Now she felt numb, saddened for the suffering her disappearance must have caused and was perhaps still causing. She must find them and explain that she was still living, that they had a grandchild. Perhaps Emily would make up for the disappointment they had felt in her. But first she must get out of this place.

Her separation from Emily was hurting her more than her bruised body. But she had to be pragmatic. At the moment she knew Emily was safe and that would have to suffice. Anja was wonderful with children and would take good care of her. Of course she could not possibly know those small things that only mothers knew about their children. She couldn't possibly know about leaving the bedroom door ajar as Emily slept so that the light from the hall emitted the right amount of brightness should she wake. Emily was afraid of complete darkness, even though she had reassured her that there was no such thing in the context of her room. Sometimes she'd attempted to demonstrate this by switching out the light. Then they'd huddled together like sardines in Emily's narrow bed, their eyes readjusting in unison, and she'd delighted in Emily's recognition of shapes as she began to define things around her. Even so her child's imagination proved more potent than her logic and whenever she had left the room, the cuddly toy reverted to a giant rat, the wardrobe a ferocious sea monster rising from turbulent waves to swallow her whole so that the night light after all retained its usefulness and was left in its dim surroundings rather like an electronic sentinel. For the moment Emily would have to be at the mercy of her imagination. She could not help her now.

She caught sight of her face in the dressing table mirror. It was pallid and bruised. This she could determine despite the dimly lit room. She closed her eyes and images moved over them like ghosts and after a moment disappeared. She searched for them consumed by a panic as if it was her own lost pulse. And then they returned. She had lived in Cambridge for a while, studied there perhaps. She remembered clearly now, walking through the streets and being comforted vaguely by the familiar sights, sounds and odours of students and tourists and flowers, the clutter of bicycles strewn across pathways, the rich smell of *real* chocolate from a small Belgian confectioners. She remembered wandering through university grounds admiring the elegant precision of the architecture. When it had been sunny the sunlight had reflected against the Godly figures on the stained glass creating a light that was blinding, as if, it might have occurred to the pious, from the herald angels themselves. But what of her identity? In what capacity had she been in Cambridge? Had she shared the preoccupations of those fair, ethereal, picture postcard maidens wafting down the River Cam under the Bridge of Sighs accompanied by gentle Adonis? Or better still, had she been a writer of great classics abundant on the thick, mahogany shelves of the more acknowledged book shops much sought after by Cambridge dons? Despite herself she smiled at these musings which occupied her as she lay in her bed and made bearable the unbearable, glossed over the malaise, transporting her temporarily to a nicer place.

She lay still, her aching, damaged body reluctant to move, remembering events with a curious sense of unreality, as if she had stolen their images from a scene in a film or play that she had seen years before and was now struggling to interpret - the yellow-bricked road of self-discovery. Small, disjointed glimpses of her life returned in this medley of words and images, some wholesome and wistful - daytime snapshots of childhood and puberty, scenes from school and home, others more recent, tender and at times erotic. In time she would remember and in remembering, she would reclaim her life. She thought of John. As long as someone was in your heart they were never lost to you. No manner of persuasion could ever change that. She could see their life together now, both beautiful and ugly, his paranoia and suspicions, her own bewilderment and occasional disappointment, their reconciliations, usually at night when anger and separateness were too difficult to bear. Pressed against him as they slept his pleasure at waking was heightened by her whorish accessibility. They could never resist each other. Between them there was a desperate avarice. Even now with her pain-racked body she longed for the comfort of him, for the pitch of his voice drenching her ears with its fretful love. She took up the pen in her stiffened fingers and wrote on the piece of scrap paper that lay on the bedside table.

"It's strange how much I communicate with you, almost as if you understand my soul better than anyone else. I suppose somewhere deep down, we are the same, watchful, not easy to penetrate the surface of. But enough, except to say that I miss the sight of your laughing eyes, and even signs of your neurosis. There has been so little laughter these last years. I have done little of consequence. Mainly I have tried to make sense of it all - our parting, our strange, obsessive life together. Now everything reminds me of you and it makes me want to cry. But I know that we will be reunited, that you will find me, as you always did, swimming at the bay or galloping across a deserted beach. I now wish to be found, despite the punishment it may bring. I have learned that misery, like happiness, can keep people together, that sometimes people grow so used to disappointment in others that, even when it ceases to

materialize, there is a need to provide it in themselves. It's an unhappy perversion but one that's familiar to me. This cruel separation that now seems written out long before, like the Doomsday Book, will surely end soon. I'm counting on it my darling."

She pushed the message inside the empty bottle of spring water by her bedside and smiled to herself. The message should be floating on temperamental seas awaiting a vague chance of discovery on some distant shore, not placed impotently on a dressing table in this suffocating room. She would endeavour to deliver it in the remote land of dreams.

CHAPTER 15

The sight of the sea after so many years absence caused a stirring in John Smith that drew him back, as if caught in its ebbing tide. He and Maria had lived only twenty miles down the coastline until the accident when he had moved back to Cambridge. Overwhelmed by the sensations he had for so long denied himself, he stood, mesmerized beneath the hunger cry of the gulls, the sea-salt air filling his nostrils, absorbing the swollen, blue-turquoise band in tranquil play with the few small sea crafts that decorated its surface. His still-raw nerves capitulated causing him to draw breath and settle for a moment on the small wrought iron bench by the cliff top. From this prospect he regarded the events that had led to that night over four years ago when he had spoken to Maria for the last time before she had been pronounced drowned at sea. The sea had seemed a monster then, taking everything he held dear, his future wife, his child, the life they had forged together. For a while he had sailed out alone every day looking for her in its monstrous depths, obsessed with its moods, its subdued languor, the furious storms. He had imagined her in its terrifying depths, reaching out to him, tormenting himself with thoughts of her agony, until he could face it no longer. Her drowning had been witnessed by two fishermen. They had seen her taken by a huge freak wave that had nearly drowned them all. She had been lost from sight almost immediately in the vast, black depths and no rescue had been attempted. There had been another boat too they said, but whoever had sailed in her had never been discovered and it had been assumed that they too had lost their life that fateful evening. He tried to imagine the scene now, to piece together the events of that night. Who might have rescued her and why didn't they report the incident?

The bay from which she had sailed had been notorious for cross-tides yet nothing would prevent her from sailing alone along the coastline almost daily to the small, solitary cove where she would read and bathe, returning sometimes after darkness. Often he would accompany her and the two of them would swim together long after the sun had died down. He could still remember the last time they had lay together on the beach there. They had argued that day about her sailing alone. He had wanted her to promise not to sail again until after their child was born but she was proud and had become indignant at his lack of trust in her abilities. They had both been silent for a while, digesting each others words and the air had grown heavy, as if wavering under the weight of their chagrin. The silence suspended over the restless sea, served only to emphasise the tension. In an effort to displace it he had suggested a swim. He had watched her disrobe admiring the new fullness of her and the pattern of light and dark imposed on her form by the setting sun. He pulled off his clothes in a reciprocal gesture and felt the sensation of still-warm air against his skin. He had suddenly felt supremely happy, as though their argument had been resolved, suddenly, within the small stretch of beach, without a need for words.

Now, as he stood, waiting to meet his newly discovered daughter he felt overcome with the bittersweet sensation of Maria's presence. He could visualise her there at the cove, her long, dark, saturated hair clinging to the gentle slope of her shoulders, florid lips showing a glimmer of white teeth as she spoke, the smile that had captivated him flitting loosely between irritation and happiness. Choked with emotion he struggled to recover his façade of indifference. He had no idea how to talk to children. Of course she would not know who he was. He was just a stranger who happened to know her mother. Perhaps he should have bought a present for her. But then, what would he have bought? He had no idea of the tastes of young girls. He must try to contain his anxiety. Her name was Emily. He liked that. They had not discussed names yet it had been his mother's and he found himself again feeling foolish with his emotions, fighting to retrieve the ironic and somewhat objectionable persona for which he was now reputed. He heard Anja and Rosy approach and the chatter of a small child. He turned and his eyes fixated on the little girl, her long, dark hair trailing behind her, driven by the wind and by the speed with which she drove her sturdy legs. She stopped before him and pointed. 'Is this him?'

'Yes indeed.' Anja was gasping from the effort of keeping up. 'This is your mother's friend. He is very keen to meet you.'

'Yes I am.' John knelt down. 'I knew your mother very well and I'd like to get to know you too.' He faltered slightly. 'Would that be alright do you think?' He smiled at her. She looked so astonishingly like her mother that he could barely take his eyes from her. She seemed to consider his proposal carefully and then remembered.

'She's not here. Do you know when she'll be back?'

'No I don't. But I'm happy to wait for her until she returns. I expect she's having lots of fun.'

'I miss her.'

'I'm sure you do. But I feel sure she won't leave you for too long.' He reached forward and removed a wisp of hair from her eyes. 'Until then maybe you and I can get to know each other a little bit. What sort of things do you like doing? Maybe we could go to visit a park or something? Maybe eat some ice cream? What do you think?' He was surprised at the extent of his feelings for her, this small child that he had just met. He felt a protectiveness toward her that both astonished and frightened him.

'I want to see that church again.'

'Church?' Anja looked surprised. 'But your mother never took you to church Emily. I'm sure she would have said.'

'We found it.'

'Is it far from here?' John offered his hand. 'Perhaps you could take me?'

She took his hand easily and his heart swelled with pride. 'Yes,' she said, 'I'll take you.'

It took them twenty minutes to reach the wooded area. Emily, who had been chatting happily, suddenly let go of his hand. 'It's through here.' She ran ahead until she reached the same spot where she had spoken with her mother and pointed up at the spire. They walked closer, Rosy and Anja astounded that they had never noticed the building before. Along the outer stone wall of the nave, ivy and clematis grew around lancet windows and, contrasting the beauty of this, more incongruous even than the cross, was a row of hideous gargoyles projecting from the roof, guarding grotesquely the serene beauty of the church. It struck John Smith then that it was so much easier to appreciate the beauty of a building in the countryside. In Cambridge, where he had first met Maria, there had been so many wonderful buildings that it had been difficult to comprehend them in one single, concentrated effort. Here in the countryside the church rose above all else like a magnificent centrepiece, its only competition the rural blanket of beauty beneath it. Somehow, beneath the vast body of church he felt reassured that all would be well and that Maria would be recovered, as if the gargoyles for all their open-mouthed hideousness, were breathing odes of love which floated like thistledown onto those beneath. They walked across the empty churchyard to a small clearing near the church where a grave rested. The soil around it was deeper in colour than the soil lower down the hill and the name on the headstone clearly visible.

Franco de Casiogy
Died much beloved aged 82

He had heard the epitaph before, though could not remember from whom it originated, but never before had it held so much pathos as now. Its sentiments seemed to resound on that ancient, lichened stone.

Stern faces bleared with immemorial watch
Looked down benignly grace and seemed to say,
Ye come and go incessant; we remain
Safe in the hallowed quiets of the past;

Emily, by now fed up with the lack of activity, was making her own, racing loudly and with suicidal recklessness around the graveyard, clambering over graves with flamboyant impiety.

'Emily,' Anja hissed, 'calm down, you're not supposed to be loud in a graveyard.'

'Why not?'

'People sleeping.'

Emily looked around puzzled, searching for slumbering bodies. 'I can't see anyone,' she said, more to herself than to anyone in particular.

John smiled. 'How about looking inside Emily. You might find the odd body in there.'

The weather was growing colder now and none of them were suitably attired. The hollow tones of wind purled through the yews and hedgerow amongst graves, dishevelled and abandoned and varying shapes of gorged, dark clouds raced over the sturdy, low stone wall that separated the churchyard from the surrounding meadows. Heavy rain fell onto their thin clothing. 'Quick Emily,' John Smith held out his hand to her and they began to run, 'let's shelter in the church.'

He had expected the church to be empty so was startled to find a man seated on the back row of the pews, his head bowed as if in prayer. He was a small man, dark and rotund and when he looked up briefly his coarse, unshaven features looked familiar yet estranged, like a father returning from the perils of the battlefield, the same discernible profile yet indefinably altered. The sound of their heavy shoes on the stone floor resounded but he continued his meditation without further curiosity which made John Smith feel more consciously intrusive. The church interior disappointed him. It was too vast and white paint suffocated all the stonework, adding a clinical contrast to the sentimentality of the Madonna and Child which was hung too high for feasible regard. On the opposite wall, partially obscured by the shadow of a cross was a painting of two clergymen in full canonicals, one prostrate, the other praying in anguish at his feet. There was a morbidity about the painting that he couldn't identify but which disturbed him. Despite their apparent intimacy the men's faces were full of their own private desolation. After a few moments his initial disappointment abated. The church, without its congregation seemed divested of purpose yet strangely more serene.

'What's up there?' Emily pointed to the staircase that led to the vestry.

Rosy looked up. 'It's just a room where the Reverend changes his clothes.'

'I'd like to see.'

'Another time Emily.' Rosy handed her a small bar of chocolate.

'I like dressing up.' She stared greedily at the stairway. 'I'd like to see inside.'

John Smith felt his skin touched by an unexpected wave of cool air. The aura of the place had communicated no expectation of habitation so he turned again to view the man on the pews but he had disappeared. Emily began skipping up and down the aisle.

'It's pouring outside,' Anja said suddenly, 'and I have only just put out the washing. It will never get dry now.'

John smiled in her direction. 'That's unfortunate,' he said, 'you know, rain always reminds me of tears. Pretty unimaginative I know but there it is. When I was young and believed in one I thought they were God's tears and it totally spoiled my enjoyment of splashing in puddles. It seemed almost sacrilegious.'

'Profiting from the misery of others!' Rosy laughed. 'I wouldn't worry about that, people do it all the time.'

'Yeah, broken hearts, what would the songwriters do without them? There's money to be made from misery. But then I've always understood that. Anyway,' he watched Emily, 'this is a great place. Do you both come here often?'

'Not a very original chat up line.'

'Indeed.'

'Actually neither of us has been here before. We're not religious and it's so remote.'

'I know,' John agreed, 'that's why I was surprised to see that it was occupied.'

'What do you mean?'

'The man!'

'What man?'

'The man on the back row of the pews.'

'I didn't see any man. Did you Anja?'

'No, no, no man.'

'Of course there was a man. I saw him.'

'Believe me if there had been a man Rosy would have noticed him. The man does not exist that she does not notice.'

'He was quite small.'

'She likes small.'

'And dark.'

'She likes dark.'

'Shut up Anja.' Rosy nudged her friend affectionately.

'Perhaps he came to visit the grave?' John remembered the grave by which he had paused, the lack of established growth surrounding it had betrayed its relative newness as decisively as the undiminished headstone. 'It was more recently dug than the others.'

'If you say so.'

'Perhaps we should leave now?' Even there in the church, out of sight, the sea's presence was overwhelming and it reminded him of Maria. Beyond death it seemed the one constant. He'd wondered when passing the mud-splashed cottages nearby, what the occupants did other than await the movements of the tide. 'Emily must be hungry. Maybe I should hire a boat and catch her a fish. I bet she'd love that. I used to be a fisherman for a brief interlude.'

'In this weather?'

'There is a fish and chip shop you know.' Rosy smiled. 'Anyway, I'm surprised. You a fisherman? You don't look weathered enough. Is that how you met Catherine, Maria I mean?'

'No, we met in Cambridge. That's where we lived for five years. She studied there.'

'She studied at Cambridge?'

'Oh yes.' He sat down on the front row of the pews. 'She hadn't wanted to go initially but it was her father's wish. It seemed amazing to her later that she hadn't rebelled since the idea of university had been terrifying to her, ill-equipped as she had been to deal with outside influences, retarded by a shyness that was almost pathological. Of course she changed later when she left home. She had tried to explain her fears to him but it had been like trying to shake a giant monolith. The idea of her continued education was sold to her rather as the advertisers sell their various products, appealing to the emotions by creating a consumer need, feeding upon insecurities and arousing discontent. But her father was adamant. What was the alternative for her, he'd rationalised? She was not a particularly clever young woman. She had no definite vocation and no personal charm with which to barter choice. Education, he said would take hold of her mediocrity and cut, chisel and remould it into something functional and remunerative. What the fool didn't realise of course is that there was never anything mediocre about her, not in any sense. So she studied hard and was accepted at Cambridge. It seemed crazy to her later, her complete lack of protest, her inability to take any course other than that laid down to her by her father. Perhaps that was why she became so independent. That was part of her attraction - her fierce independence. And ironically she has lost that again.'

'There's so much that we have to learn about our friend. You see, all we really know is that we love her.'

'What more does anyone need to know?'

Anja touched his arm sympathetically. 'I can tell that you feel the same. You must not worry. We will find her. Perhaps by now Santos will have discovered something.'

'I hope so.'

They moved toward the entrance which, ajar, volunteered a small section of verdant landscape. Outside the rain had stopped and the air, purged of its downfall, was clear and aromatic. Emily followed gaily, stopping briefly to consider the staircase that led to the vestry door. She wanted with all her longing to see beyond it, to feast her eyes upon the ceremonial garments marked with strange insignia like the ones in the painting. When they returned to the path John put her on his shoulders.

'That's my house there.' She pointed toward a group of trees that seemed to John Smith for a brief moment, to be separated artificially by a thin, convoluted wisp of wood smoke from one of the chimneys. Then it dissipated like a will-o'-the wisp. The house, grey and melancholic, glared back at him, he thought, with an air of dissension. They had already visited the farmhouse, he and Santos. They had broken in through a rear window. He had desperately hoped to find her there or else, her jailer, crouched fugitive-like on the floor of the oak-panelled room, to beat into submission. But inside the house had been uninhabited and dismal, had echoed the stark melancholy of the night. Upstairs he had seen where she had slept, had smelt the heat of her. 'It's strange,' he had said to Santos as they made their way back to the cottage, 'when I walked into that room where only hours before she must have slept, I was thinking, of all things, of the breadcrumbs, hers and mine, the very distinct types of hard and soft that she once so lovingly carried to me on a plate. We'd brush them off the sheets - no longer food, except for thought - mmmm night food.' It was strange to think of those crumbs somewhere deep in the carpet pile or inextricably woven in the weft of her strewn clothing. Perhaps there had been some at the farmhouse too.

Emily was tired after visiting the church. When they reached the cottage, John Smith read her a story until she dozed and he carried her to bed. He could hardly bear to be parted from her. Each time he looked at her he could see something new of her mother about her. Downstairs Hilda shuffled about restlessly. 'I could do with some cake with this tea,' she twitched.

'You've only just eaten Hilda. Do you not remember? We had a large feast to welcome our new friends.'

'I wish I could remember where I'd put it.'

'What? The bird?'

'No, my Bible.'

'You don't read the Bible Hilda.' Rosy winked at Anja. 'In any case I have one at my place. You can have that if you like. I don't need it.'

'It's not the same.'

'*Ach Ja,* they are all the same. They all speak of God and Jesus and disciples and such things.'

'This one's got a picture of Pal George and Bill Shed in it.'

'In the Bible?'

'Yes, I put a photo in between the pages to stop it bending.'

'Oh, I see.'

'I want some cake with my tea.'

'I don't think we have any.'

'Would you like me to fetch some?' John Smith rose reluctantly from his easy chair. He too felt tired from the journey and the emotional disappointment of finding no traces of Maria. 'I can drive to the nearest store.'

'That is not necessary.' Anja moved languorously toward the kitchen. 'I believe we have some cake left over from Christmas as it happens. I will fetch some for everyone.' Moments later she returned carrying a tin with a snowman design on it. She took the top off. 'Oh dear, it doesn't smell like Christmas cake.'

'It smells a bit strong,' Hilda wrinkled her already crumpled nose, 'did you use the same ingredients as last year?'

'I have never tried British Christmas cake,' Santos leaned forward to observe the aesthetics of the cake, 'but why have you wrapped it in newspaper?'

'I remember now, I remember!'

'What Hilda?'

'Where I put him.'

'Who?'

'Twinkletoes. I've just remembered.'

Anja dropped the tin with a faint squeal and the small, decomposed body of a bird fell deftly from last month's news.

CHAPTER 16

That evening the sea seemed restless, as though echoing the mood of the inhabitants of the cottage set in the hillside. Waves broke noisily over the rocks in the bay as they swallowed the dark sands with a ravenous hunger. Santos was already bewitched by the place, as he was by the woman who now walked side by side with him in this remote idyll. She had taken his arm as they negotiated the footpath toward the cliffs, quite naturally, as though they were one of those ancient, weather-beaten couples who had spent a lifetime together in the whitewashed cottage and were just taking their habitual, nightly stroll. She was funny and made him smile, from time to time roar with laughter before she remembered what had brought them together and then her eyes stilled and sadness subdued the curve of her mouth.

'I have told you my life story,' he said slowing their pace, 'or at least the significant parts... how I drove my wife away with my preference for research, what a neglectful husband and father I was. So what about you? What ghosts lie in your wardrobe?'

'Nothing much to tell,' Rosy shrugged, 'I live alone with my daughter Lucy. We're very close but she's very independent and as you can see, spends most of her time at Anja's. My husband was too traditional for me and too selfish. He kept saying that our marriage could work - we were both sentient beings he said, over and over till the phrase stuck in my throat like a fishbone. It was always like that. He was the one who talked about trying and I was the one who tried. Give me back those eight years or at least seven of them. I could use them more constructively now that I'm older and wiser. Youth is wasted on the young as they say.'

Santos laughed. 'I'm not sure that's true but it is likely that by the time we recognise that particular banality for what it is, we too will probably be old and it will profit us to carry on the imposture.'

'Oh GOD,' Rosy threw up her arms in mock horror, 'please NO, don't let me be old yet. Let me enjoy this newly-found wisdom, apathy, nonchalance, for a few years yet while I can still, as Travis put it, "*get 'em fired*," turn the heads, if not like spinning tops then like taps, even stiff, uncertain ones.'

'Who is Travis?'

'My last boyfriend. Oh, another thing I should tell you about me is that I have a habit of making bad choices, at least as far as men are concerned. Always too young and never the sharpest knives in the drawer, if you know what I mean.'

'And Travis was one of these?'

'"Life is a journey," I used to tell him, enjoying my comparative wisdom. "A journey from optimism to cynicism. When you have mastered both, the world changes colour. In fact you can pick your own from the spectrum, or even don the coat of *many* colours." Do you know how long it took me to think that up?'

'Was he impressed?'

'"*Cool*," I think he said, before popping another ecstasy tablet in his mouth. He used to call himself a writer though he lived on benefits. He used to sit there pressing blotting paper into the small pools of ink he'd deliberately spilled to give himself an excuse not to write. It could never have worked.'

'No, I confess it doesn't sound very promising.'

'I should probably have married Toby,' she said wistfully. 'I really loved him and we were such friends. Friendship is so important in the long run isn't it? But he used to go out with prettiest girl at my dance class. Her name was Kathy I think. She threw him over for one of the dance instructors. That's when I saw my chance. I went to lunch with him at the Ghengis Khan Mongolian Bar-B-Q and asked him if it hurt. "Only the first time," he said to make me smile. "I've traversed into another era of my life, that's all."' She grimaced. 'Unfortunately it didn't include me.'

'You liked him a lot?'

'He was so philosophical and apparently unafflicted. There was only one time when he allowed me to see his vulnerability in the raw and that was after he'd watched a programme about fishermen harpooning whales. He cried then, a single tear and said, "Is it my imagination or is the world going to hell in a hand basket?"'

'Very deep.'

Rosy laughed, 'It seemed so at the time but then I was only sixteen. I was easily impressed. I still am.'

'And your family, do they come from around here?'

'No, from Kent. It's almost as beautiful there as it is here, but not quite. This is home now.'

'I can understand why. But how did you get to be here?'

'Ah, my ex. I have to credit him with that. I met him at Reading in Berkshire where I went to university. Well, polytechnic to be exact, for those slightly less academic students, not quite dismissed as factory fodder but nearly. I studied Art and Design there though I can't remember much about it now. When I wasn't studying I used to spend all my time on buses, just watching everyone outside, shopping and zealously pursuing careers. That's what I did for fun. I was a people watcher, a consumer of passing words like FLATS TO RENT and HUNTLY AND PALMER'S BISCUIT FACTORY, CLOSED UNTIL FURTHER NOTICE. I was an odd girl really, and distinctly unattractive. And of course just to rub salt in the wounds I had to get the most gorgeous room mate. You know the type, blonde and well-stacked. I used to idolise her, bought into her image like a fan might buy a souvenir ashtray or some other piece of kitsch. She was a complete bitch too and as thick as shit but God was she popular with the boys.'

Santos laughed. 'We men can be very superficial. So then you met your ex-husband and moved here?'

'Not immediately but yes after a few years. He carried on studying for a bit so I got a job for a while rather than go back to Kent to live with my parents. Mum insisted that I wrote every week though, all through poly, which as you can imagine was quite a chore given that, as I said, my only hobby was people-watching from the giddy heights of double-decker buses. I remember having to resort to writing things like, *"Reading is famous for freak whirlwind deaths once every 1,900 years,"* hoping this might conciliate her.'

They had reached the beach by now and Santos pulled her suddenly toward him. 'You know I don't think anyone has made me smile so much in years. You make me want to behave slightly crazy, not like me at all.'

'Well,' Rosy smiled, 'if that's true then prove it.' She kissed him playfully on the lips and then stood back and began to take off her clothes. 'Let's swim.'

'Are you mad? It's evening. The water must be freezing.' Santos was feeling the effects of her kiss. 'Let's go back to your cottage.'

'Not until we've had a swim.'

'You crazy girl.' He laughed loudly but followed her lead until his clothes lay next to hers on the damp sand. His body was thinner than she had anticipated yet his shoulders were broad and surprisingly muscular. The motion of his bent arms threw a darkness over the convexity of his chest and the muscles in the lower part of his body tightened as he bent forward, forming a rigid curve. Here her eyes rested, devoid of subterfuge, watching the heavy pouch of darkled skin move forward with the sway of his hip, his excitement for her obvious even in the darkness - the pull of the tide, she joked. Moments later they surrendered to the ceaseless motion of the sea, their bodies, greedy now, alive with a protracted craving, until the heat of their beating flesh drove them to the shore leaving them beached and spent.

Later as they lay in bed in Rosy's dimly-lit room, Santos stretched contentedly, studying her athletic form, miraculously taut despite her self-confessed idleness, her sea-salt flavour still sapid on his tongue. 'Tonight has been very special for me. I haven't felt this good or this close to someone in years.'

'Always glad to oblige.'

'I mean it. I am not usually so demonstrative.'

'It must be wine-induced.'

'I haven't drunk any wine.'

'Must be the sex then. Hey, one night with me!'

'Are you ever serious?'

'Only when I have to be. Life's too short.'

Still heady from their intimacy Santos rose unsteadily to his feet and fetched a small black briefcase from the far side of the room. 'I thought you might like to see this. It is a photocopy of course. I could not risk losing the original and of course it is far too delicate.' He passed her the A4 sized paper.

'This is in Spanish.'

'It is.'

'Then I think you might have to help with a translation.'

Santos laughed. 'Of course, of course. Come close to me and I will read it to you.'

Rosy studied the unfamiliar words. 'I don't understand. Is this one of the letters you found?'

'Of course. You can see it is addressed to Goya and signed by Alba.'

'And do you think it's authentic?'

'I do.'

'This is unbelievable.' Rosy noted the quill-formed words which spun dizzily around the page. 'Read it to me, please. First in Spanish so that I can imagine her sounding the words as she wrote them, then in English.'

'As you wish.' He took up his reading glasses from the bedside table.

"Mi Amado Goya,

Quizás sea por mi condición pero me desperté esta mañana con un presentimiento. ¡Cuánto necesité en ese momento que me abrazaras y consolaras! Pero claro que esta imposible situación nos impide hasta los más mínimos placeres. Algo tendrá que suceder para resolver esta situación. Pero no debo de ser morbosa. Cuando nuestro hijo nazca nos tendrán que aceptar y estaremos unidos para siempre - - dos corazones latiendo como uno.

Pero como el tiempo pasa ociosamente, fatigado por la impaciencia y cobardía y la convicción que yo nunca tendré el privilegio de envejecer. Una muerte sin gloria, ya que mi simplicidad no permite un legado de genio más allá de la tumba. Tú, mi solo Goya, reclamarás la inmortalidad. Tú viajarás sin esfuerzo a través de los siglos, a través de ascuas de carne quemada, las ruinas de grandes ciudades que hacen ecos de las pesadillas que has vivido, los gritos de los familiares mundos perdidos que resuenan del pigmento que sólo tú podías colocar.

Parece que nosotros trabajamos hacia nuestra muerte, en buques dañados y rotos por las lecciones que hemos aprendido, corazones fatigados por las guerras del amor y principios, plagados por los espíritus que susurran de nuestros indecibles crímenes de sus tumbas no marcadas. Si con suerte todavía hay ternura y compasión en nuestras corroidas almas. Esto, temo, es todo lo que puedo dejar a mi hijo. Pero haciéndolo puedo reclamar mi propio pequeño renacimiento, una llama de vela, no parecida a la cual escribo ahora, pero una llama que no se puede extinguir porque amó demasiado bien.

Siempre tuya, María"

'And now for the translation.'

"My beloved Goya,

Perhaps it is because of my condition but I awoke this morning with a sense of foreboding. How I needed you then, to hold and reassure me. But of course this impossible situation denies us even the most commonplace of pleasures. Something must surely happen to rectify the situation. But I must not be morbid. When our child arrives they will have to accept us and we will be united forever - two hearts that beat as one.

But how time idles, fatigued by impatience and cowardice and a conviction that I will never know the privilege of growing old. A small inglorious passing, as my simplicity allows for no legacy of genius beyond the grave. You, my only Goya will claim immortality. You will travel effortlessly through the centuries, through the embers of burned flesh, the ruins of great cities echoing the nightmares you have lived, the screams of lost, familiar worlds resounding from the pigment only you could place.

We work toward our death, it seems, in vessels damaged and broken by the lessons we have learned, hearts fatigued by wars of love and principle, plagued by spirits whispering our unspeakable crimes from their unmarked tombs. If lucky there is still tenderness and compassion left in our eroded souls. For this, I fear, is all I may have to leave my child. But in so doing I too can claim my own small renaissance, a candle flame, unlike the one by which I now write, that cannot be extinguished because it loved too well."

Rosy was silent. Despite their remoteness she felt oddly defeated by the words so providently and resignedly written. She imagined Alba, in her fearful isolation, forming her self-fulfilling prophesy on the sepia page, the man she loved absent and forbidden. Then she thought of Catherine, trapped for so long by her limitations of memory, estranged from her grieving lover and the pathos of Alba's words deepened like a love that returns to haunt through the cobwebs of antiquity.

CHAPTER 17

Screams resounded through a darkness almost impenetrable and dismal glimpses of the tortured bodies of two men and a woman illuminated the dungeon. One of the men's intestines spilled loosely from his gut onto his thighs as he dangled from tall chains. The other was devoid of his limbs which hung suspended like a debauched, spinning mobile above his head. Bleeding profusely and near to death, he wailed himself into oblivion. The woman too was beyond help. She had been gruesomely raped and was bleeding from every orifice. Her wrists which had been tied behind her stripped and broken torso disallowed modesty which, even in her grave agony and after the indignities she had suffered, she sought to regain. What could these poor souls have done to deserve such a fate with the inquisition? They had probably been proclaimed heretics and witches for some farcical offence, some small eccentricity that had sealed their fate. The woman turned and he saw with horror that it was Maria's face.

John Smith awoke, perspiration dripping from pyretic flesh. His head was a fusion of tangled images, of Maria, of Goya, of towers that imprisoned, of drownings. He must find her. But where? It was like trying to decipher the complexities of hieroglyphics. He felt an odd burst of hilarity, the type that sometimes pervaded at funerals when the solemnity of the event became unbearable. His head was still buzzing from dreams, but this time full of burlesque verses - lace and suspenders and high kicks. One must have kicked him between the thighs because when he tried to speak his voice had changed pitch. His body felt chilled now, and his lips were blanched from the cold, his fingers frozen to the phalanges. What was he doing in this room, loitering, like a whore without custom, while she remained unfound? He switched on the bedside light and looked at his watch. Time seemed to be standing still. Then he realised that his watch had stopped. He poked it, blew into it, took off the back and manoeuvred the cogs but to no avail. The hour remained unmoved. He fastened the watch around his wrist anyway. The strap was too tight, because of the missing link no doubt. He prayed it would be provided before time ran out.

Rosy and Anja could provide few insights. 'Catherine was, *is* I mean, a very private person. She doesn't really do trivia, you know, all those details that employ the gossips for weeks. That wasn't her style. And that's one of the things we love about her. Her life is devoid of narrative. She's one of those rare individuals who lacks a profile, or at least one that she could refer to and she was all the more interesting because of it. She was an innocent really, learning about life through others, very intuitive and self-deprecating, but not communicative. And she never mentioned *him*. It was as if he didn't really exist, or at least, as if she didn't want to be reminded of him. With us she could enjoy a little escapism. Call it respite.'

'You never saw him to speak to?'

'I saw him at times, like I said, from a distance. At least I assumed it was him, big, surly, walking near her farm. I used to see his car in the village. He was, well, you know, shifty. I imagine he was up to all sorts of shady deals, always off to see a man about a dog, that sort of thing.'

'*Na, Ja,* Rosy is correct.' Anja looked solemnly into John Smith's penetrating blue eyes. 'You could feel the sadness in her. Why should we spend our precious time together increasing this? She enjoyed our foolish banter, tales of Rosy's flirtations, the children's antics, but she gave away very little. And now because of this we have no way to help her when she most needs us. I really think that it is soon time to involve the police.'

'No we can't panic him. Who knows what he's capable of?'

'I agree,' Rosy looked sternly at John Smith, 'but not for too much longer. If we can't trace her soon then we have to inform the police. Agreed?'

'Just give me a couple of days. I don't want him to be alarmed. He's a man who is in danger of losing everything and there's no one more dangerous than a man who has nothing more to lose.'

'You could ask the local Reverend if he could tell you anything about him. They always make a point of knowing their parishioners, even those less than devout.'

'*Ja Ja,* good idea. He will be giving a service soon in the village, at the church with the four points.'

'Points?'

'She means pinnacles. Most of the churches around here have spires. This one just has a tower.'

'Then I must find it and see what this Reverend has to say.'

'Do you expect to find Catherine locked in the tower like Rapunzel?'

'Don't be ridiculous.' But he remembered the strange hypnotic quality of the Bourgeois towers with their suggestions of enclosure. He imagined her there waiting for him in her seclusion, her long, dark hair trailing beneath a Gothic window arch.

As if reading his thoughts Anja said, 'I have painted an impression of Rapunzel with the wicked witch climbing up her hair. It was influenced by the work of Arthur Rackham but of course my version is louder, much louder.' As if to demonstrate the reverberant quality of her paintings she erupted into a sonorous belly laugh. 'Perhaps there is something in all women that relates to the idea of being locked in the proverbial tower, just as there is something in all men that responds to the notion of war.'

'Not me. The dogs of war can cry havoc elsewhere. I'm just an old pacifist with a healthy interest in self-preservation.' He searched for his jacket. 'See you later. Who knows the vicar may remember him. Jesus, we're not talking about the invisible man. Someone somewhere must have seen him or know of his whereabouts.'

'It's worth a try. I'm going back to the farmhouse with Santos. You may have overlooked something. We'll take Lucy and Emily.'

'Emily can come with me.' His words were driven by a pathological fear of Emily's abduction.

'We'll take care of her. Don't worry.' Rosy was uncompromising in tone. 'She wants to go home and get some things. She still has all her toys there. She doesn't understand what's going on or where her mother is. I think she needs to see for herself that the house is deserted.'

'And I will make lunch and look after the kids and the crazy mother-in-law. And of course wait for your friend Griffin, though I don't understand exactly why he is coming.'

'I told you, he wants to see your work. Never look a gift horse in the mouth Anja. Your paintings have an original quality with their rhythmic lines and violent colour. The right agent could make you a lot of money. That's something Griffin certainly has a talent for.' John Smith smiled. 'He'll have you as the reincarnation of Dali before you can say Salvador.'

'*Accch*, I would NEVER prostitute my talent in that way. If art is good then it stands on its own merits. I could never do what you have done. It is undignified.'

John Smith smiled at her affront. 'I think you'll find that everyone has their price Anja. There are some artists who literally can their own shit for publicity, or display their menstrual knickers. Welcome to the world of art.'

'Not me. I would NEVER do anything for the sake of attracting public interest. That kind of attention does not interest me.'

'No one's incorruptible. You'll have your price just the same as the rest of us.'

'*Quatsch!* Nonsense!'

The church was not difficult to find. Standing high on the cliffs, John Smith could view the whole panorama. At least four churches could be seen and only one embedded in the heart of the village that failed to boast a high spire, like a poor, squat relative to its slender sisters. He arrived just in time for the service which he found not simply dull but dispiriting in that it relied heavily upon the deference of no more than a dozen people who, having arrived, ensconced themselves in isolated positions down the aisles as if to create the impression of fullness. Either that, John Smith thought, or they couldn't tolerate each other. Absorbed by his commitment the rector delivered his sermon, happily devoid of cant, from a carved, oak pulpit with a passion undeterred by the derisory numbers. John Smith watched, his face steady and bright, framed by light hair as his words broke into the balmy silence, and wondered what his own presence there signified. He felt divorced from the rest, encumbered by sin and guilt which would surely be observed if he made a conspicuous move or breathed too heavily before the organ moaned into its next hymn. The pews were hard and cold and his limbs ached with an urge for movement. The lights in the church seemed too bright causing his vision to blur and beads of perspiration to break onto his forehead as though he was being exorcised of his sterile and angry denunciations of God. The Reverend's mouth now formed its shapes in silence and suddenly the congregation was moving forward, sipping wine that posed cleverly as blood, shed for the remission of sins. He retreated into the daylight, disorientated, a feeling of sickness numbing his dry limbs. Shortly afterwards the congregation began to disperse. The Reverend glanced in his direction before moving toward a nearby headstone where he knelt and tended to the weeds with a nearby trowel. John Smith moved toward him, then, noting his look of despondency which momentarily surpassed his own in terms of importance because it had a grave to represent it, he moved inside the church. He was suddenly unsure of the wisdom of his visit.

'May I help?'

John Smith turned.

'Can I be of any assistance? I couldn't help noticing your presence during the sermon. You appeared to derive little comfort from it.'

'That's true,' he eyed the Reverend suspiciously, disconcerted slightly by his candid approach. 'Despite the silence engendered by fat walls and the absence of telephones, a church is not the ideal place to seek solace. At least not for me.'

'Me too, at times,' the Reverend smiled, 'though I suspect the congregation here would be offended by that declaration, at least, coming from me.'

Just what the world needed - a trendy vicar. Despite his stillness he had, John Smith thought, a theatrical presence about him. His cassock looked ill-fitting, as though it had been hired for a costume drama. He reminded him of all those unknown actors playing Hamlet at Stratford, eager to make their mark by being original, yet so original that they were often unable to support the grandeur of the story. 'I'm looking for a man,' he said clumsily. 'He lives in a farmhouse two miles north of here with his wife Maria, I mean, you would know her as Catherine. You would have noticed her. She's very beautiful, has long, dark hair and a young daughter called Emily.'

'Of course I remember her. Even in these parts, or perhaps I mean especially in these parts, beauty like that is a rarity. But I don't think I've ever met her husband. In fact I didn't know she had one.'

'I see.'

'She bought the farmhouse nearly five years ago. I distinctly remember as she purchased it from a friend of mine.'

'You mean a little over four years. And the house would have belonged to her husband.'

'No, I remember distinctly her buying it. She got quite a bargain. And she had some fine plans for it as I remember. Some kind of artistic retreat, the next Charleston perhaps? You know that house lived in by the Bloomsbury Group? The farmhouse is such a tired looking place I looked forward to developments, but none of them reached fruition. She seemed to change when she moved here. She'd lost a lot of her *joie de vivre*, couldn't remember our previous conversations, was very reluctant to communicate at all in fact. Look,' he noted a hint of consternation, 'if you'd like to talk maybe I can help?' He remembered the face of the woman very well. She had stood out amongst the tedium of usual faces like a tragic Madonna.

'Thank you but no. My only interest in being here is to determine whether you could help me to locate this man but it seems that he's undetectable. And I've disturbed you, dropping by like this without appointment.'

'It's not a dental surgery.'

'No, of course.' John Smith continued somewhat self-consciously. 'You see, I need to find my friend as soon as possible. I fear for her you see.'

'In what way?'

'This man, her husband. I fear he may be holding her against her will.'

'And why would he do that?'

'For love of course. Why else? Why else would someone risk their livelihood, their reputation?'

'Hatred? Jealousy? Revenge? Love can't be the only inducement.'

'Huh, they're all derivatives. In any case,' John Smith shuffled uncomfortably, 'it's a long story.'

'I have plenty of time.' The Reverend gestured to the pews and discreetly closed the church doors behind them. Small lamps lit various sections of the church which had seemed foolishly extravagant given the natural sunlight but since shutting the church doors the interior had darkened considerably. John Smith had always liked dark spaces. He had worked in a dark room once when he was a student. His job had been to feed film into an automatic developing machine. It might have been extremely tedious work but it had had the attraction of working in complete darkness where his thoughts had had the space and quiet to grow. Here, however, the darkness had an eerie, premeditated quality to it and his companion seemed too keen for details.

'Please feel free to tell me anything you want. You say you've lost your friend?'

'She disappeared. You see she lost her memory just over four years ago. I thought she was dead but then we were briefly reunited. Then she ran away.' He was aware his words were garbled and incoherent and felt the same level of discomfort he had felt during the sermon.

'And why would she do that?'

'Shock I suppose, in confronting her past so uncompromisingly.'

'*Uncompromisingly?*'

'*Suddenly* then.'

'Shouldn't finding yourself be a positive experience? It should have been a happy moment of revelation surely?'

John Smith felt intensely irritated. 'Like the first time a clergyman realizes he fancies the choirboys?'

'That was unnecessary. I realize you're a little overwrought but I'm just trying to help.'

'I apologise. But I'm sure it would have proven to be a "*happy moment of revelation*" as you put it, had she stayed around long enough.'

'But she didn't.'

'What are you trying to say exactly?'

'Nothing. I'm just trying to help you to recall, to make sense of it all.' He paused, uncertain whether to proceed. 'You're an artist aren't you?'

John Smith sighed defeated. It was sad that he had felt a need to fabricate, but sadder still that the truth itself seldom impressed since honesty demanded so much more courage. And now he had reached the depths of degradation, sitting in this faded church with a man whose whole life was almost certainly a lie. An artist saw the truth in a man's face, he could see the torment of each line and shadow, each droveway of shame and regret. 'Tell me vicar, are you married?'

'Yes but I don't see…'

'Then you will know all about lies.' He could imagine him now, kissing his wife perfunctorily at the doorstep that morning, a faint, bridled kiss. She would probably have been oblivious to his face, stricken with a weary resignation before it became animated once more, preoccupied with his male lover, their clandestine meetings, his perverse excitement at the prospect of their deception.

'I was just trying to raise a mirror to your face, help you work out what may have happened to your friend. There was no ulterior motive. I'm not about to try to convert you. I can see that would be a waste of your time and mine.'

John Smith eyed him with some scepticism. 'I see? Well, I suppose it's good to know that the door is ever-open, and that - even in this present, unsympathetic climate of, let's see, economic recession, homelessness, violence on the streets and in schools, a criminal justice system that doesn't work and a health system that's a national disgrace, not to mention all the parishioners that are suffering bereavement and struggling with their faith - you still have enough energy left to listen to the inane ramblings of a man who claims to be the reincarnation of Goya, but I think I'm wasting your time Reverend.'

'On the contrary.' Mistaking irony for encouragement his face brightened a little. 'I don't feel that my time is being wasted at all. You see, for me the principle source of fascination about a person is reflecting on their inner mental condition, discovering their experiences so that I can put my finger on the pulse of their creative inspirations.'

'I'm afraid the last of my creativity has just drained away Reverend.'

'I'm sure that's not the case.'

'Tell me Reverend, and forgive the digression, but why is your service not held at the larger church in the woods - the one with the magnificent spire? It has such a sense of sobriety about it. It's within your diocese I believe.'

'You've been there?'

'Yes. There was a man sitting on the rear pews when I entered.'

'What man?'

'Small, dark, oddly familiar. He didn't speak, just sort of disappeared. One minute he was there and the next minute, gone.'

'No one ever goes there except me.' The Reverend's voice had a sudden curtness about it. 'It must have been the ghost that you saw.' He laughed nervously. 'The church was deconsecrated, sold to a private owner at about the time your friend bought the farm. But whoever bought it has never appeared to claim it. They probably had in mind to turn it into some ghastly conversion. I can't say I approve of that but it was out of my hands. In any case the place closed for Sunday service long before that. People thought it was haunted. Too many sightings of ghosts I expect. Not that I'm a believer but it's indisputable that some places have a presence about them. It's so overgrown now that I'd assumed no one would ever find it. I should keep away from there if I was you. The place has a bad feel to it, an ungodly feel.' He stood up stiffly and said in a final attempt at civility, 'An interesting *Madonna and Child* though. Unusual. I've considered bringing it here but I've never got around to it.' Just then the church doors opened and a man in his twenties with epicene good looks greeted them with a smile so broad and superlative that John Smith was uncertain momentarily from where the sudden rays flooding the room originated. 'Well, I'll leave you to your ruminations. I'm sorry I couldn't have been more help.' He nodded to the young man and they left closing the door discreetly behind them.

John Smith lost sense of how long he sat there thinking. Despite himself some of the Reverend's words had resonated and he found he could not easily dismiss them. He must try to remember the night that she left, the events that led up to her departure when she was lost at sea. He did not want to remember that night but would much rather he thought, contemplate their mornings, how nice it was to lie in bed with her and what little justice was done to the very ideal occupations of the unemployed. Why had she run away from him? The Reverend's question had stung and he found himself submitting to a downward spiral of introspection which intensified with each unbearable moment. Jealousy was a monster, an unimaginable monster. He felt himself buried in a deep, deep hole. He could feel it caving over his head at times as thoughts unravelled, feel his demon limbs tussling with the ancient shards, his inner juices ejected from injured eyes. The Reverend had been insistent that Maria had bought the farmhouse herself and before her disappearance. What could this mean? Suddenly he knew. When he returned to Anja's cottage that evening the sun had descended without warning so that when he looked through the car mirror there was only a shimmering half globe of reds and oranges to record its recent departure. The concept of its return the following morning seemed difficult to grasp.

CHAPTER 18

Charcoal fed deftly through Anja's fingers capturing the mouth, black, hollow and agape, like a cave without stalagmites and stalactites, from which dragons might at any moment breathe fire. Hilda looked particularly cadaver-like in repose, devoid of teeth, the unforgiving sun displaying the ravages of time without mitigation. She was, Anja thought, like a living *memento mori*. She snorted into consciousness. 'Did you bury Twinkletoes with Albert like you promised?'

'I did Hilda.' It was a foolish promise to have made but one that could be broken without the threat of revelation and Anja, besieged by young children and consumed with fear for her friend, did not possess the necessary energy for confession. Her thoughts were interrupted by the sound of a car drawing onto the pebbled driveway.

'It was the dwarf in the roof that did it, that killed Twinkletoes I mean.'

'What dwarf Hilda? The bird died of natural causes. It was an old bird you know.' She had been expecting John Smith's agent so was surprised to see her husband's car.

'The dwarf in the attic. It has a skunk to keep it company. I caught them you know, shooting dope, putting hydraulic acid in the water cistern, sorting through Albert's letters and trying to frame him. Evil both of them.'

'Of course they are Hilda. But don't worry about that now. Your son is back from his travels.'

'He's no son of mine. He's the dwarf. You want to stay away from him.'

'Just a moment Hilda. You stay here and I will put on the kettle. Stay and watch the children for me.'

She stood. Her husband was approaching slowly as if with some trepidation. She noticed for the first time how silently he walked, the only visual distraction the long strand of hair that was strategically brushed to cover a bald patch and which made constant and vain attempts to fall, licking his eyelid until flicked deftly back to within its boundary. When he spoke his voice seemed higher and more circumspect as if he had sustained in his absence, some contamination to his vocal chords.

'Hello Anja. You're looking well.'

'George, you are back early. I was not expecting you for a few days. Come and say hello to your mother. She was just talking about you.'

'I'm not staying.'

'No? You are leaving so soon? But the children will be so disappointed.'

'They won't even notice that I've gone. Or you either for that matter.'

'What do you mean? You are looking so serious.' She turned to check the children. Hilda was trying to chase them in a series of arthritic-ridden twists and turns that produced what looked like a modern hip-hop version of a *Danse Macabre*. The children squealed hysterically indifferent to their father's arrival. 'I was just about to make some tea.'

'I'm leaving you Anja.'

'You are?'

His voice returned to its usual pitch. 'Yes, I've been offered some work on the east coast.' He eyed the children sheepishly. 'I probably won't be back to these parts for some time.'

'Oh, I see. Well, perhaps we should talk about this?'

He made an attempt to smile and she noticed that his crooked teeth were still festooned with remnants of his last meal. She hated dirty teeth. 'Sorry old girl but I started divorce proceedings some time ago. I said we'd already been separated for quite a while.'

'Oh?'

'No point in dragging things on once we've made up our minds.'

'*Our* minds?'

'Well *mine* then.'

'And the children? And your mother?'

'Look. You can take care of them. You're a born nurturer Anja. And I'm leaving you the house.'

'But the house was mine before we married.'

'Well, that's what I mean. The house is yours. It's not as if you won't have a roof over your head.'

'I suppose you have withdrawn money from our accounts?'

'Well, I have to live on something.'

'How much?'

He said nothing.

'You've taken everything haven't you?' His silence spoke volumes. 'I see, and how should I be expected to feed everyone and to pay the bills may I ask?'

'Look, I'm sure you'll find a way. You were always the resourceful one. You could take some of those paintings of yours to the car boot sale for a start. Somebody might take them off your hands.' He added absently staring at the children in play, 'There's no accounting for tastes.'

'I see.' Anja paused. 'And what is her name this time may I ask?'

'*Whose* name?'

'The woman you are leaving me for.'

'Look,' he turned impatiently, 'there's no point in any scenes. I just need to collect the rest of my things.' He turned away and then, as if troubled momentarily by his conscience he paused. 'You have a nice life here Anja, tinkering with paints, surrounded by kids. And my mother's always around to talk to.'

'She has dementia.'

'It takes her a while to fathom things that's all.'

'Oh *Ja,* like your father's death. She was still attempting to feed him after three days. He had Brussels sprouts coming out of his ears.'

He smiled. 'Best not get bitter eh? It doesn't suit you. Pragmatic, that's how I think of you.'

'Still there are things that need sorting out before you go.'

'I'll write when I have an address.'

'You know that is a lie.'

At that moment another car drew up and Griffin waved in her direction. 'Anja?' Behind her the children wailed in affray and now Hilda too lay prostrate, shrieking for assistance in the grass. Anja glanced cursorily at her husband, the unruly children and the approaching stranger, uncertain who deserved priority but her legs in any case seemed unable to facilitate movement. She heard her husband fart, a belated and distant *non sequitur* before he disappeared into the cottage and she turned to Griffin's outstretched hand.

'You must be Anja.' His eyes followed hers into the distant cottage. 'I hope I haven't arrived at an inconvenient moment?'

'That's my husband. He is just leaving me.' Despite herself she felt a sudden paroxysm of panic.

'Oh dear. John always said that my timing rivalled that of Lord Cardigan's.' Anja looked uncomprehending. 'You know, *The Charge of the Light Brigade*? "Into the valley of death rode the six hundred."' He shrugged, 'Never mind. Should I leave? You must be in a state of shock?'

'*Nein, nein.* I need some help to pick up the old lady.' Hilda was still writhing about on the grass much to the amusement of the children. 'I swear she falls more often than the children but she never seems to do herself any damage.' She smiled at Griffin. 'Perhaps there is no more damage to do.' She took his arm. 'And then I will make you a cup of tea and show you the paintings. That is what you are here to see *Ja*?'

'If you're sure.' He eyed the cottage uncertainly, not sure how his arrival might be interpreted. 'Is John around?'

'He has gone to ask the Reverend a few questions which may help us to find Maria. He will no doubt be back soon. And Rosy and Santos have gone to her house to look for traces of her. I only hope that they discover something soon. I am so worried for her. She is like an innocent you know. She has so little idea of the world.'

Hilda's grey hair was covered in freshly mown grass. 'Has he gone yet?'

'Who Hilda?'

'The dwarf.'

'It wasn't a dwarf Hilda. It was your son George.' She gestured to Griffin. 'She is not, *wie sagt man,* how does one say, *not the full shilling.*'

'I see.' He helped the old lady into her seat. 'About your husband. Don't you want to talk to him? You don't seem too upset, if you don't mind me saying.'

Anja shrugged. 'The truth is I am a little dazed. And at the moment there are more important concerns.' She shrugged with a nonchalance she did not feel. 'In any case there is something liberating about knowing the worst of people. And once you have accepted it there can be no more disappointments. Ah, here are Rosy and Santos and the children. Maybe they have news. I will put on the kettle.'

'Have we got any cake?'

'You and your cake Hilda.'

'Don't give any to the dwarf.'

'It wasn't a dwarf. It was your son George.'

'Did he have the skunk with him? Did it smell?'

Rosy and Santos had discovered nothing and Emily, fractious, went straight upstairs.

'She kept saying that she wanted to go to the church to see her mother.' Rosy sighed, 'I kept trying to explain that she wasn't there. She's so confused poor lamb.' She pointed to the car in the driveway. 'I see that George has returned.'

'Only for the moment. He is leaving me.'

'My God,' Rosy lit her first cigarette in years, 'that's the first time I've known him to show you any consideration. But I should make the most of it if I were you. No doubt he'll be back when his latest infatuation runs its course and he runs out of money.'

The shift of focus from Maria to Anja was a welcome one for Rosy who, tired and disillusioned from their fruitless quest was beginning to believe that she would never see her friend again. She had used the spare key that Maria had given her to enter the farmhouse, her hand shaking its reluctance so that she dropped it twice onto the mulch beside the doorstep. The house had an atmosphere of desertion about it beyond emptiness, a stale and odourless nothingness that had disclosed none of its secrets. She had climbed the stairs. She had only visited the house once before and had never noticed how severe they were and how leaden her gait when ascending them. The air too felt heavy and difficult to swallow, as if primed with pollution, pollution of the baleful kind. She searched not knowing what she was looking for, discovering only the simplicity of her friend's life and little that reflected the furnishings of her character or determined how her life had unfolded. It was as if, along with its deafening silence the pulse of the house had stopped beating, grown wearisome of its own vacancy. It seemed to her at that moment the saddest place on earth. She did not notice the diary left carelessly on the bare boards of the sitting room, antique in colour and camouflaged well. It was Emily who noticed this and, thinking it pretty, added it to her collection of toys. The words in it she could not decipher but there were many empty pages that she could draw on. And if she held it to her nostrils and breathed in deeply it smelt still of her mother's touch. She had at times seen her writing in it with that abstract look that she reserved for the quiet evening hours.

'It's just, well, you know Rosy, how I struggle with change,' Anja sighed. 'If only Maria was here, his departure would seem less upsetting.'

'One must embrace change if at all possible,' Santos added with conviction, 'life is not a static thing. Otherwise our lives become impoverished by our own cowardice, our own neglect and we never discover our full potential. We remain incomplete.'

'Albert was incomplete.'

'In what way Hilda?' Anja refilled Hilda's cup of tea.

'His testicles never descended.' Her face was expressionless. 'At least they hadn't the last time I checked but of course that was some years ago now. The doctors said it was a miracle that I got pregnant at all. And I was forty-nine at the time. I thought I was going through the change.' She hugged her meagre bosom. 'Of course it would be Sod's law if they dropped now when no one wants to see them. They might as well drop *off* now.'

'Albert's been dead for years Hilda. Don't you remember?' Hilda said nothing.

'You see,' Anja added pertinently, 'Hilda too finds change difficult.'

'Anyone who can paint like this,' said Griffin, gazing at the walls around him, 'can change the world. They are remarkable paintings Anja. Tell me, who is the girl in the tower?'

'Rapunzel. But of course in my painting she is mixed with other images.'

'Seemingly disparate images. But they aren't. Symbols of purity as in ivory towers melding into the distant landscape. Very surreal. They show great talent. And your imagination has extended your paintings beyond purely technical competence. I have a very good feeling about these. We must arrange a show as soon as possible. Tell me how many canvasses do you have?'

'About fifty or sixty. There might be a few early ones in the attic.'

'Excellent.' He smiled at Anja. 'Your life might be due for another change sooner than you think.'

'*Achhh ich weiss es nicht*. I don't know. The problem is I have always had a fundamental mistrust in my own power to effect one, a change that is.' She looked through the window at the burst of colour outside. 'But it is possible I am sure. Look at the garden. Have you ever planted seeds and watched in awe as they transform themselves into beautiful flowers? The first time I planted some I could hardly believe my eyes. And it is the same with people. You are right. We can make things change and change for the better if we open our minds to it.'

'Albert doesn't like change. He says it doesn't matter where you put your cross, politicians are all the same, only concerned with lining their own pockets.'

Griffin could hardly draw his eyes from the paintings but added abstractedly, 'She must have loved him very much to be so convinced he's still alive.'

'No, she is just mad. CUCKOO mad.'

Rosy discarded the cigarette. 'Like Dali?'

'Dali wasn't mad. He was quoted as saying, "The only difference between a madman and me is that I am not mad." You must have heard of his paranoiac-critical method? The artist simply tricks himself into going mad, always aware that he's doing this in order to create paintings as opposed to suffering true insanity and all that that entails.'

'Hilda doesn't paint.'

'Yes,' Santos grinned, 'but imagine what such a mind would produce if she could. You should visit some exhibitions of Outsider Art.'

Anja opened a bottle of wine. 'I am finding tea a little sedate at the moment. I think we will have an early drink.' She was grateful for her sudden exhaustion as it meant that any reasoning that might have led to a remote analysis of her day was absent.

'Of course Anja you must be feeling wretched. Whatever you think of him now you must have cared for him once.'

'*Acch Ja*, I should have taken more notice of those first impressions. We met at a friend's birthday I remember. He was wearing a T-shirt that said PARTY ANIMAL on it. When it was time to leave he just said, "Call me," and turned to piss out of the window. *Na Ja*, things never really got any better. I remember him asking me where I wanted to go on our honeymoon. I'd always wanted to go to the Grand Canyon. There's a place there that you can fly over to see the most magnificent views so I said, *Point Sublime please*. He said did that mean that a good shag would do. I thought he was joking. But the worst was…' Anja's voice drifted with endless tales of dissatisfaction resurfacing like battleships for further bombardment. The others listened as she continued her exorcism, indulging her bitter reminiscences, allowing the dry, stale crusts of her marriage to break away bit by bit into the midnight hour. The darkness outside became complete, the moon stolen by clouds which opened to release their cleansing rains as if to wash away the grief of yesteryear as easily as they might the sad made-up face of a clown.

John Smith arrived back at the cottage shortly before midnight. Without conference everyone had been awaiting his arrival which brought with it a weighty, dreadful expectancy, a last vestige of hope. His face, the dull colour of stone negated any such optimism. He sat by the pot-bellied stove in Anja's kitchen, his head in his hands and for some moments said nothing. How could he explain the inexplicable? How long would it take? A lifetime? Or as long as it took for the water closet to refill? He said, 'Maria's husband doesn't exist. He's a jealous ghost, a misnomer, arisen, not through misinformation but pure speculation. He's a Chinese whisper, a product of the grapevine, as hollow as a jungle drum. The man you saw on the camera was no doubt just an innocent passer-by.'

'Don't be ridiculous. Of course there's a husband.'

'Did you ever SEE him? Did she ever REALLY speak of him, other than indirectly, as one might personify an emotion or …' he searched hopelessly, 'a cancer?'

Upstairs Lucy was carefully colouring the pages of the diary that Emily had brought back from the farmhouse. The words meant nothing to her but she liked the slant of the writing. She turned to the last entry and began to draw a frame around the letters.

"For the last four years I have lived with a ghost. Not one of those tired apparitions that lighten darkened corridors of Gothic mansions or those that speak of more enchanted days. My fears and failings lock me in my uncomfortable skin, my own walled city of confusion, while He sits back in the broad shadows of my half-remembered demons and laughs. He sleeps in my bed each night, my incubus, his jealous congress arousing me in the early hours. He reads my shallow thoughts and adds his own. I am his muse, his Melpomene and He is

my jailer, feeding me the rotting fruit of his obsession. My life seems spent throwing pebbles into nebulous pools and trying to determine where the ripples go. Will it find me again, this life or will it remain obscured from view like paintings hidden in caves for centuries, their meanings now lost or indecipherable?

Tomorrow I have a chance to escape this limbo, to discard the ghost of my own manufacture - for all our ghosts are surely generated by those inexplicable fragments of knowledge we have accrued, by the experiences we have sustained, the trials we have endured through fate and circumstance, by enemies whose motives we can't control, by friends who care for us despite ourselves and by lovers whose bodies become like familiar and beloved landscapes. But these atoms of life that make us up can also disassemble us, can curb each tender remembrance with shadows cast from our imperfect histories. All I want is to liberate myself from the shackles of ignorance, to discover a life without fear, to wake in the company of partisans."

Beneath the words Lucy drew several matchstalk men in skirts with smiley faces. Emily's bed was empty. She had gone to the church to see the painting of her and her mother. She had wanted to go earlier but Rosy and Santos wouldn't take her. So she had gone on her own. Lucy knew instinctively that this would displease her own mother and she awaited her imminent outburst as she heard her footsteps on the stairs.

Chapter 19

Emily was cold and rather frightened but determined to continue her short yet monumental pilgrimage. By night things looked different and she wished that she was not alone, that her mother was by her side. She wanted to hum a tune that her mother had taught her or to try to whistle but the sound of her own voice in an otherwise unpeopled landscape would have unnerved her. She was close now. She had reached the cluster of trees and she walked beneath them afraid to look up. The trees were so large and they had grown larger in the darkness. Perhaps they had faces. Perhaps their branches would turn into arms and sweep her up. The church loomed ahead, consistent with the trees, taller, assuming its own personality. She had arrived at its arched door and wondered if she ought to knock but this seemed foolish so late at night and besides the door was already open. She placed a foot cautiously inside. She had waited an eternity to see the painting of her mother again and the room upstairs that they called a vestry. She had been patient and had given Rosy and Santos the time and space that adults seemed to require to listen and respond. She had wanted to ask more often, but had not, had recognised in her intuitive, childlike way the need for patience. But earlier that day Rosy had promised to take her and her sense of injustice was profound. 'I feel so tired now Emily. We'll go tomorrow. Please don't make a fuss there's a good girl.' Emily had fought back her tears and felt a momentary hatred of Rosy for not understanding. Her mother would have understood and she would never have broken a promise. She needed the reassurance of seeing her mother's face again, even in a painting. She also wanted to see the vestry and the garments, like those in the picture high on the church wall. The men in it had captured her imagination with the colours and textures of their gowns so rich and decorous. She wanted to see their faces again, to understand the strangeness of their expressions, to pull similar robes around her small frame and feel the fabric, slightly abrasive against her skin. She knew that she would be protected by the virtue of the cloth. She had heard in school assembly of a church called the Church of the Veil where the robe of the Virgin Mary had been taken and had protected a whole city from being conquered. Apparently when the robe had been placed into the sea it had caused huge waves that had destroyed all foes. If holy robes could save cities then they could easily save her mother and bring her home. Thoughts of it made her fears evaporate, fears that her mother would never return, that she would be left alone in the hostile world of schools and adults who didn't understand the importance of important things. She began to cry, but inwardly, so that she did not make a noise and her tears ran down inside her head instead of the outside. She felt them tripping over the Adam's Apple in her throat depriving her for brief moments of air. Tonight she would find the robes and bring one home, not an extravagant one that might be missed, but one like the holy virgin wore, she who was never pictured without her child. She would look at her mother's face on the church wall and make a wish and then she would find this simple, special cloth and she would climb into her mother's bed with it at the farmhouse and cover them both so that they would never, ever be parted again, not ever.

A whisper of light illuminated a vague notion of distance that prevented her from tripping but the nave of the church was too dark to view the objects of reference that might assuage her fears - no pews, no lectern or gentle contours of her mother and herself high on the ochre, stone walls. She could hear noises now and they frightened her but she kept moving toward the vestry unable to stop. In her short life she had never felt so tangibly in danger. What was that noise that grew louder with each step? Perhaps someone was dying, was being murdered? Perhaps they would kill her too? She drew to a halt beneath the smaller arch of the vestry door. It was open and the angle of its openness threw her into a shadowy purdah. The men did not see her. Their arched and frantic shapes projected mammoth images onto the wall from the light of one candle and it was from these images that she withdrew as if their magnification consolidated the greatness of the danger. It was then that she screamed, a small, diluted scream that echoed strangely as she turned in her red, buckled shoes and ran out into the darkness.

In her fear and confusion she did not consider direction but ran as fast as she could out of the church, voices calling from behind her like ghostly threats in their echoing surrounds. Her small, slight, bare legs snagged and grazed in the swollen undergrowth, tripping over the roots of the giant trees that knotted the earth beneath the soil as if in an effort to lift her into their folds. Above too, these giants fought for space, branches in leafy canopies that locked her in a terrifying darkness, obscuring any exit from their ebony maze. In her short life she had never before experienced terror. She could feel her heart pound, the blood rise to her dry throat as she ran forward deeper into the wild wood. Trunks of varying girth trapped her in their mass, passing her from one to another as if in a cruel game. Weak with anguish she fought her exhaustion, bravely scaling the steep banks of earth toward the distant comfort of the whispering sea. She had no idea how close she was to the cliff edge or how many from countless generations before her had plunged to their deaths in the deadly silhouette of that ancient and uncultivated thicket. It was not as she thought, the mouths of bears or wolves that waited to devour her but the gaping mouth of the sea crashing its readiness onto the rocks beneath, awaiting the next victim with the certainty of time immemorial. Her small, red, favoured shoes slowed as she fought her way still through the tangled network of oak, lime, birch and pine, of privet and dogwood, of bramble and nettle. Her bare legs stung violently with pain soothed only by her own sweat and blood and urine, diluted by the heavy rainfall which now penetrated the leafy umbrella above. The sea called to her again. It was closer now, singing its welcome as she dodged the last of the forest giants which swooped like drunken villains, dripping wine from their great boughs.

She could see light flickering through the darkness and hear the poetry of the waves rising and falling in their seductive rhythm. The light of freedom glimmered like a sword lifted from its scabbard into the open skies. She was free. It was then, as she moved toward the cliff edge only feet away from a certain death that lightening struck and it was with this advantage and due to the heightened watchfulness created by her fears that she saw the man's figure. He held out his arms barring her way, his face distorted by fear and it was then that she saw the water beneath her, restless and unforgiving, beating upon the jagged rocks. She looked up but the man had gone. She knew his face. He was the man who had been sitting in the church on her first visit after her mother's disappearance. He had a kind, old face. She turned. She could hear voices now calling her from further along the coastal path.

'Emily don't move. Please don't move.' John Smith walked slowly toward her. Rosy followed behind him her hands raised to her face in dread. 'It's okay now Emily. You're going to be fine. Just don't move. Don't look down.' The edge of the cliff began to crumble slightly and several inches gave way. John Smith reached forward and caught her small, fledgling-like figure, raising her tenderly into the safety of his grip. He had no idea what had made her stop at that crucial moment, what premonition had halted her ruby steps. He had watched with horror as he saw her tiny shape emerge from the spinney and race toward the precipice and though his heart had cried out his voice was silenced in agony. Yet she had stopped.

There was a folkloric belief amongst the sailors of some coastal towns that the sirens who lured men to their deaths with their seductive melodies, also had it within their power to protect the most innocent and brave of sisters. Or had it been the seabird of good omen, the Albatross, "*in mist or cloud, on mast or shroud*," sent by the ghost of the Ancient Mariner to steer her clear from the tyranny of seas? Or perhaps some other, unsung spirit?

CHAPTER 20

The awakening hours brought with them a quality of calm that held fast, as if anchored in the silent seas and in the still air. Like a curse that had been lifted from a sleeping village, the weariness had gone and life at the cottage resumed with a milieu of optimism, doubts and fears exiled like a ship of fools to a far-away place, to some other distant, grieving heart. The journey to the church that morning was in stark contrast to that of the night before, as if mood and motive could alter, not only the sensation but the appearance of the world. Could that ghostly coastal path, chastised by both sea and storm, be the same from which this tropical warmth now emanated? Could the fears that raged over man and beast in that dark wilderness have so readily and gracefully retired? John Smith carried the young girl to the church basking in the knowledge of her safety, reassured by the small but shifting weight of her on his back.

Anja and Griffin stayed at the cottage, Griffin desperate to view the extent of Anja's work. His eyes possessed that look of singular animation that John Smith knew only too well. His plans were already manifest, discernible in his brow and stance and tone of voice. He had discovered another triumph. He had known the moment he set eyes upon Anja's paintings, just as John had. Of course they were not as accomplished as

John's but there was something fresh and rudimentary in them that promised to ripen, something exciting. She was his own *Alfred Wallis*, the tiny fisherman turned painter who had been discovered by the sophisticated St Ives Group, painting his naïve images of ships on pieces of driftwood and anything else he could acquire. No doubt everyone had laughed at him then, his childlike images, his limited palette, an art illiterate they would have said, as well as one of the ordinary kind but he had persisted in his beliefs, remained true to himself. *"There have been a lot of paintins spoiled by putting Collers where they do not Blong,"* Wallis had famously written. Now all Griffin had to do was to consider how to promote Anja, find out where she *'blonged'* in the world of art. Of course, she was not untrained but she was a complete unknown which gave him more latitude. It had also occurred to him on his journey from London that since these latest developments John was in no state to fulfil all his artistic commitments. He had another television interview in a matter of weeks that he had not even considered and as far as his exhibitions were concerned he had nothing new to show. He needed more time to resolve these issues before he could commit fully to his painting, that much was obvious. There had to be some sort of conclusion and soon. He too, despite himself could not dispel the sense of intrigue that clung like the scent of lavender to the cottage walls. Ever since he had arrived in this strange, excessive place Griffin's perceptions too had lacked certainty, as though parts of his mind were becoming entangled in the strange, wild landscape. He was a city dweller. He understood the hustle and bustle of London, the congested impatience of its streets, its focused industriousness. But this landscape confused him. It drugged him with its sleepy patience and lack of industry. Like an inattentive host it left him to his own brooding meditations which for him was anathema. But its undeniable beauty captivated. He felt its addiction and observed it in John. It had taken the edge off his malevolence which he didn't approve of. It certainly wasn't good for the reputation he had spent time and money cultivating. Next he would be kissing babies and helping old ladies across the road.

'What "felonious little plan" are you contriving in that money-obsessed brain of yours you miserable bastard? I've seen that look before.'

Griffin smiled reassured. 'No matter. I think I was worrying unnecessarily.' He watched his friend depart like the Pied Piper accompanied by Santos, Rosy and an endless stream of brightly dressed children. Hilda remained, marooned on her bed, cheated of the emblem of her eponymous appellation, *Granny Peg Leg*. Griffin had observed a couple of the boys earlier hiding her prosthetic leg in the garden with the feckless cruelty of children, great guffaws of laughter piping the tranquil air and causing their treacherous hearts to beat like drums. And though he had heard her pleas for rescue he was determined to overlook them until he had settled certain matters with Anja who he recognised, even in the short time since his arrival, would have spent this rare and precious time liberated from her children, pandering to the demands of the ancient woman. He amplified the volume of the radio, drowning Hilda's lamentations with the rebellious sounds of some obscure rock band.

The coastal path, newly golden with sand and sunlight led its occupants once more on their small pilgrimage to the church of noble spire. Of equal nobility the trees of the bosky wood outstretched their limbs as if in welcome, lush, dewy leaves reflecting the new tenor of the day. Emily eyed nervously the section of the cliff path from which she had nearly fallen. Here the path narrowed, perilously close to both the cliff edge and the clearing that led through the trees, down the soft, grassy bank toward the church. The whole experience of the night before now seemed like a bad dream and she could barely determine which parts were fact and which fiction. Perhaps she had imagined the voices and their great shadows? Or perhaps they had been echoes of ghosts, long dead awoken by the tapping of her red shoes on their restless graves? At first she had not wanted to return but the brightness of the day, the reassurance of numbers and the broad back upon which she leaned and drowsed made the journey a fearless one. She was desperate now to see the painting of her mother, a comfort that had last night been denied. The sweet aria of the blackbird stood out amongst the vain chitter of finches. She could feel the essence of her mother in the distant whisper of the sea, the cotton-clouded sky and most especially in the man who carried her on his back, quelling her fears with his reassuring presence. He in turn was enslaved by her evident faith in him, by her endless bale of expressions which she practised on him without guile or premeditation and which broke his heart for the occasions he had missed. The painting was there high on the wall as she had known it would be. From her new perspective she could view it more clearly, she a small baby, cradled in the arms of her mother whose maternal devotion exuded from dusky eyes.

John Smith stood transfixed. He recognised his own work, but drowsily, as one might an old friend in unfamiliar territory after years of estrangement. He was confused. Did this mean that Maria owned the church? She had received inheritance enough to do so. Had she meant to convert it into a gallery? A church was not the ideal space for artistic communion in his eyes and any conversion would have to deal with more than impediments of light and space, but the revenant spirit of centuries of devoutness cloying an enlightened post-modern audience. He had given Maria the painting in anticipation of Emily's birth. He would never forget her delight in response to it, as though he had fulfilled a long-desired wish or offered reassurance to some unspoken doubt. As far as he had known she had stored it with her other paintings until she found the perfect place to exhibit them but after her disappearance he had been unable to locate it. It made sense now. She had wanted to surprise him. He remembered her animated expression as she had spoken of her trip to another part of the coastline. Her absences had caused him some distress but when he had confronted her she had been so elusive that, even in her gravid state he had become convinced that she was seeing someone else. Finally he had spat out his accusations, vicious and untimely while she lay swollen on the sheets beside him, blue sheets the colour of the sea with glimmers of white foam on their surface, the light in her eyes growing dimmer with sadness at his mistrust. When she finally slept he had stayed awake, sick with suspicion and shame. He saw those same eyes now, beyond the love for her child, none sadder, eclipsed by the weary resignation of someone who had lost all faith.

He could hear the incredulous gasps of Santos and Rosy behind him and caught vague passages of their conversation, his thoughts of Maria too deep to withdraw totally to the natural world. Despite his affection for them he wished he was alone with Emily at that moment. It was as if the others were intruding on a world which belonged to him, as though the secrets of the painting and his life with Maria were revealed simply by its exhibition, those private, sacrosanct moments of lovers violated by exposure. 'When will she come home?' He heard the whisper, soft yet urgent upon his ear.

'Soon,' he promised, 'very soon. I expect she's on her way right now.'

'How do you know?'

He considered for a moment. 'Because your mother's free now. And free things have no need to escape.' They moved outside the church and he put her down on the soft grass. 'It's like those birds you can hear. Put them in a cage and they lose the will to live, but if you release them then they will fly to the branches beneath your window and sing to you all day. And sometimes it's the same with people. Even though they aren't really in cages, it feels like they are. So they have to sort of fly away to sort out their thoughts. And then they come home again because the things they love most are waiting for them, like you.'

'Do you have any birds?'

'No, but I have a cat with China eyes.'

'Does it speak Chinese?'

'I don't know. You can ask it if you like.'

CHAPTER 21

Hours before Maria had made her way to the roadside where she had raised her arm like a bow at the passing traffic. She had been released from hospital that morning and her body, though still traumatised, ached mostly in a need for home. The man who had knocked her down had visited her daily, already in love, repining his slow response at the wheel despite her reassurances that it was her own fault. She had not been concentrating, had been distracted by the ringing of the telephone, by the muffled confusion of a head well-populated with unwanted voices. He had wanted to drive her home this dark, enigmatic woman, to discover more of her but when he had arrived that morning she had vanished without trace, like smoke into the atmosphere and despite their brief and formal acquaintance, he had felt cheated of something he could not place.

She had hitched a ride all the way to the Cornish coastline and now she turned from the growling truck, waved goodbye to its driver and wandered to the beach where she abandoned her shoes, allowing the heavy syrup-coloured grains of sand to grip her feet in protracted motion. She approached the sea with languid steps and the sea reciprocated, barely lapped so that their meeting was a cautious one. The water was cold only initially and had soon seduced her to thigh depth. She realised with the abruptness of a strange truth that since that night she had never bathed in the sea. She wandered down the coastline with this thought, enjoying the gentle pull beneath her as the tide withdrew and then released, taking with it some of her aching.

She said goodbye to the sea. In return it beat out one of its familiar, well-documented rhythms that gently tugged at her tall, slender legs, as if attempting to lure her back into its subtle traction. How calm it seemed, a new face after its night time exertions no doubt. How different it had appeared that night and how easily she could have been spewed up onto its brink with the morning tide like a piece of driftwood. Its omnipotence somehow rendered the dry land and her existence on it parochial, yet still she felt her veins transfused with a new energy that might, she dared hope, translate to happiness.

High above two figures negotiated the steep decline of the coastal path. Emily, still tired from her night time adventure was content to be carried once more. Above her gulls circled in the drowsy air. She watched them, her lazy thoughts returning to the church, the painting and the small vestry room which had been disappointingly empty, devoid of the magical clothes she had desperately sought out. There had been no trace either of the ghostly shapes locked in anger that had shaken the sturdy walls. But the sight of the painting had reassured her and it was this image that she clung to now, as tightly as to the sturdy shoulders, afraid to let go lest the memory of her mother's gentle smile should fade. She closed her eyes, yet still silent tears escaped onto John Smith's neck and shirt. There was nothing sadder he thought, than inaudible tears which kept their heartache locked in private mourning, spilling grief in their unexpressed concerts with no expectation of consolation. Yet he wanted more than anything to console her, to share her sadnesses as he might her successes, with a paternal pride that it was him in whom she confided. He felt a need to be alone with her now, to be singularly responsible for making her smile again, to labour for her, to build her intricate castles with moats that the sea would laughingly destroy and he then rebuild. Whatever was broken he would always repair for her. He would be happy to spend the rest of his life rebuilding her sand castles. They parted from the others, making their excuses and the other children, florid cheeked from play followed Santos who was talking excitedly to Rosy about Goya and lost paintings and how they must return to Spain immediately.

As John Smith turned with the meandering coastal path, a strange phenomenon occurred. The scene before him changed suddenly from day to that of a nocturne, the colours of the seascape instantly dulled. The small splashes of colour that he had earlier noted had suddenly turned monochromatic as if by magic and ships he had observed on the horizon had disappeared in a shroud of darkness. Even the wail of the gulls seemed subdued by the inexplicable eclipse. It was as if winter had changed its mind and boycotted spring, regaining its benighted powers that obscured the clarity of day. The sea had ceased motion, was dreaming of a new day and the only movement was of a figure, small in its distant perspective, moving leisurely across the dark sands. In that instant he knew, and, paralysed by both joy and terror he stood, any other sounds silenced by the painful beating of his heart.

'Emily.' He shook her gently from her melancholic slumber. 'Look.'

The small girl strained to adjust her eyes to the new light. When she saw the figure on the beach she let out a small shriek of pleasure yet made no attempt to climb down from his back. Instead she dug in her small, red heels excitedly as though he was a lazy mule that needed to be urged into a reluctant canter. 'Hurry, hurry,' she reprimanded. She began to wave her short arms and to call out to her mother in her loudest voice yet it had begun to rain and a wind, incited it seemed by the genie of the sea, howled in salty indignation so that her cry was inaudible to all but the closest of companions. Yet still the woman beneath stopped and looked up, her flowing hair caught up in the genie's censure and though John Smith could not see it he could sense her glorious smile.

CHAPTER 22

There was nothing muted about the colours of Sanlucar de Barrameda, the sky a clear, cerulean blue, the buildings iridescent white, reflecting a heat that was rich with the scent of orange trees, tapas and Manzanilla sherry. The journey from Jerez had passed by in a cloud of easy sensations that transported Rosy, as if by a magic carpet, past the vineyards, the pine forests and the aureate beaches. The town was situated on an estuary where the great Guadalquivir river reached its final destination and was swallowed languidly like a fine wine into the gullet of the great Atlantic which in turn was ingested by the motionless sky on its distant horizon. Rosy listened happily to Santos's stories of the town's history, of how Columbus had once left from Sanlucar port on his journey to the Americas and of how the first Duke of Medina Sidonia had come into power in the thirteenth century, converting from his Muslim faith in order to further his political ambitions. Goya's mistress Doña María del Pilar Teresa Cayetana de Silva-Álvarez de Toledo y Silva, had been the thirteenth Duchess of Alba and allegedly the most beautiful woman in Spain. Though much loved by her people she had powerful enemies including the Queen of Spain, Maria Luisa de Parma, a woman as plain as the Duchess was ravishing and who many believed had conspired to have her rival poisoned for usurping the affections of her lover Manuel de Godoy. Others believed that the perpetrators were servants who stood to benefit from the Duchess's fortune. Even now in the old quarter of Sanlucar at the Plaza del Cabildo, people sat beneath the orange trees at the cafes and bars drinking the local wine, in heated debate about the mystery surrounding the Duchess's life and death. There were those who believed that her affair with Goya had been little more than a rumour, an ailing man's fantasy, and that the inscription *Solo Goya*, Only Goya, discovered during the 1950s restoration of the painting *The Black Duchess,* implying the Duchess's devotion, was simply Goya's way of coping with unrequited love. Others believed that theirs was the love of ages, an eternal flame that burned steadfast, as ancient as the civilization of Tartessos, as steadfast as the Castle of Santiago. And there in the heat of that magical place Rosy was inclined to believe the latter. She sat in the Plaza del Cabildo by the cooling fountain, like a pulse circulating its stream of nostalgic curiosity and wondered who this enchantress had been, so full of contradictions, tender with the young and infirm yet with a lust for matador blood.

Even in death, she continued to mystify. Sometime after her demise she had been exhumed and it was discovered that one foot had been severed from its leg. Could this be attributed to superstitious ritual, the Queen's obsessive jealousy of her rival's well-turned ankles or the practicalities of fitting the Duchess into an undersized coffin? She felt herself drawn deeper into the mystery. Somehow this woman, as charismatic in death as in life, had become synonymous with Maria. The similarities between both women were uncanny, not just in their physicality but in their ability to obsess, which seemed less connected with their haunting beauty than to a certain aloofness of spirit. The ordinary and the commonplace did not belong to their world, she understood this, their lives were unencumbered by the limitations imposed on ordinary mortals, their days as long as they arranged, time an endless possibility.

Despite all her friend had been through she couldn't help envying her. Her own life, in comparison, was gauged by duller edifices. She smiled wryly at her own shortcomings. There were no works of art to represent her. The occasion of her own daughter's birth had been marked only by the absence of her spouse, later recovered from the local bar "as drunk as a fiddler's bitch." Yet here she was in Sanlucar de Barrameda searching for a lost Goya painting which recorded the Duchess of Alba and their noble, bastard child. Santos was convinced that the painting had for centuries escaped discovery due to its guise as a Madonna and Child, just as John Smith's painting had hung in the forgotten Cornish church, unquestioned and mostly unobserved. Rosy was not so sure. This was not helped by the fact that she had very little idea of what she was looking for in the many and varied Spanish churches. Of all her company she understood art the least. Would the Duchess be enthroned complete with halo and traditional blue mantle? Would she be in the form of an altarpiece, a fresco, a canvas? And would the child be passive and suckling, the usual type of religious iconography? She thought this unlikely given Goya's horrific painting *Saturn Devouring his Son*, which wasn't a good indication, she thought, of paternal devotion. Santos had been amused by this. 'That's different,' he smiled, 'all connected to the Greek myth of Cronus. Nothing at all to do with Goya's personal feelings about paternity.' He noted her look of chagrin. 'But of course that is good logic on your part. The kind of logic that I will need to help me find this painting.'

'I'm not remotely logical. Do you know when I was a child at school I wrote that if I was a fish I'd want to be a sardine cos then I'd be in a tin and no one would be able to get me. Does that sound logical to you?'

'Perfectly!'

The Church of Nuestra Señora de la O neighboured the Palacio de los Duques de Medina Sidonia, the Duchess of Alba's former home, but despite its numerous chapels it appeared to hold no secrets within its Mudejar-style walls. Stepping through its great Gothic-arched doorway Rosy noted the stonework above depicting heraldic lions. If only they could speak what tales would they tell of former congregations, of spirits both temporal and eternal? The pews, simple wooden structures, seemed at odds with the great, gilded retablo which appeared both breathtaking and obscene in its opulence. Rosy felt out of her depth, the iconography of the place addled her brain like a foreign tongue. Carvings and devotional figures were omnipresent - in the alcoves, the chapel screens, the pillars and walls. She studied each work of art under the carved wooden ceiling with an unfamiliar intensity resting momentarily under the ornate dome that hovered above like a giant halo, pronouncing all those who walked beneath it saints. So many paintings each more complex than the other. Santos explained the symbolism of the skulls in the *Deposition*. There on the hill of Golgotha Christ was lowered into his mother's frail and weeping embrace. Rosy felt that the gold in the painting detracted from its sentimentality. Too much gold and too many halos. She paused at a painting of *Saint Sebastian*, like a strange *Pinus nigra* with his arrow branches piercing his bloody sap. How acutely concealed seemed the rewards of martyrdom. There was only one *Madonna and Child*. It looked at first to Rosy like any other representation she had seen, Mary swathed in a blue mantle holding her newborn child. The Madonna's face was beautiful but did not look particularly like the images of the Duchess she had seen, the skin too olive-toned, the eyes too heavily-lidded. Santos paused beside her. 'Competent but truly unremarkable. Far too conventional for Goya. It shows none of his passion, his vision, his energy.' The gilt frame seemed too ornate for the relative drabness of the painting yet Rosy reminded herself that it was old, its true colours obscured by centuries of dust and heat. And there was a true serenity to the Madonna that Santos had overlooked, keen only to discover in the craquelure the secrets of age and provenance. To him the painting was of no consequence, was invisible. Like a woman grown old whose allure had died he dismissed it without sequel. It was Rosy who studied the canvas, the cherubic child with his arm raised in benediction, his gaze toward the viewer, the Madonna passive and detached, eyes turned from her offspring in silent meditation. The canvas was slightly damaged near the centre, the paint raised and at one point on the Madonna's face a small fragment had broken away. Perhaps it was not considered important enough for reparation or perhaps its decay was considered part of its charm? They moved on, looking upward, dull of spirit, to the three-tiered belfry where the melodious echo of bells in worship had just subdued. A version of *The Last Supper* hung high on the second level, the twelve disciples responding in expression to the news of Jesus' forthcoming betrayal.

'We must not lose heart,' Santos said unconvincingly. 'The painting is here somewhere. I'm convinced of it.' He looked around him. 'Perhaps this church was a little too obvious. It was really absurd of me to think that such a painting could remain unobserved for so long in this of all places.'

They continued their search for several days unsuccessfully. Rosy soon recognized the need to look beyond the features of the church where expectations of battlements, balusters and arch-braced roofs gave way to Renaissance paneling and Moorish portals. Despite these differences the spirit that arose from their consecrated grounds united them in centuries of worship. But the secrets of the Spanish churches remained embedded in their framework like death-watch beetles. Santos began to speculate as to whether an undiscovered crypt hid the Goya painting. Rosy privately wondered whether it had ever existed. She lay awake on their penultimate night fatigued by the preoccupations of both sex and supposition. Too tired for sleep she reached over to the bookcase, knocking a small book onto the stone floor. She picked it up and turned to its open pages. It was a small English Bible. She read, "*And the Lord said to Abraham, Look toward the heaven and number the stars, if you can number them.*" She was reminded of the painting, *Saint Francis Standing in Ecstasy*, St Francis's upward gaze as if to some distant Arcadia. Occasions for numbering stars were coming to an end. Tomorrow they would leave for England. Like an ancient Babylonian sundial time was losing its face.

She lay awake in the darkness, a sense of urgency bearing heavily, like an overweight lover, upon her slight frame. Based on the premise that the painting existed, the question was no longer where it was hidden but how? Despite her limited knowledge of art her powers of observation had become heightened these last days through invariable scrutiny. And besides, a painting was not an inconsiderable object, unless of course it was a miniature and, though Goya had painted miniatures they were not plentiful. So it wasn't as if they were looking for the proverbial needle in a haystack, yet the walls of each church and palace, though rich with art, showed no signs of Goya's hand. What was the secret of the painting's crypsis? She must think laterally. In nature creatures avoided detection by camouflage like soldiers in combat. As a child you hid your secret thoughts with invisible ink and unseen stamp marks allowed you re-entry into dances when viewed under ultraviolet light. Yes, disguise was better than concealment - a secret place would eventually be found but who would discover the true identity of the man behind the mask? These thoughts incubated in the heat of night until a fledgling of an answer began to form, flap its tender wings and take flight. At the moment of realization she felt foolish rather than clever, as though the delay was due to some inadequacy in her thought processes rather than a moment of inspired deduction. But when she awoke Santos to tell him that she knew the whereabouts of his missing painting, though it sounded like an apologetic triumph, it was one he was no less thankful for.

CHAPTER 23

The serene yet pedestrian *Madonna and Child* was removed from the placid walls of the Nuestra Señora de la O after nearly two centuries and delivered to the Rutherford Appleton Laboratory in Oxfordshire, England where it was examined by a team of forensic scientists, art historians, restorers, authenticators and the Diamond Synchrotron whose ultraviolet beams penetrated deep into the bones of the painting to reveal the masterpiece beneath. The magnificence of the hidden painting was beyond all expectation, the face of its tragic goddess, her beauty still unrivalled, staring out from beneath the veneer of a fair yet less enchanting gaze. It was easy to see, Rosy reasoned, why the Duchess of Alba was considered the most beautiful woman in Spain despite the absurdity of such a concept which was as ridiculous as saying that a particular dish was the most flavoursome or a favoured tune the most melodious. None of the Duchess's features were flawless yet there was something in their arrangement that suggested they were, a small but significant deception emanating from something more primal and altogether more interesting than perfection - some fancy or proclivity from the heart or loins or a complex mixture of both.

The painting stayed at the laboratory for several months, the complex operation of removing the top layer of paint without damaging the composition beneath demanding the utmost skill and patience. The use of the chemicals which determined the speed at which the paint was removed was exacting and Santos waited like an expectant father as the patina of dull pigments was eradicated. With surgical precision layers of lead chromate and red iron oxide were lifted from the face of the canvas revealing the subtle tonal gradations of the Duchess of Alba and her child. The painting was officially and undisputedly pronounced a Goya, priceless and scandalous by implication and in conjunction with the letters, secured Santos new veneration within the world of art. To him though, most compelling of all was the striking similarity of the painting with John Smith's which had hung, similarly overlooked in the Cornish church as though dissimulated for some exalted purpose and without which he would never have discovered the truth. He spent many lidless nights in contemplation of this phenomenon.

*

Meanwhile, morality, so easily weakened by poverty, had abandoned Anja with the subtlety of an earthquake. Her form engulfed the burgundy leather sofa of the television studio, pursy calves shifting across each other, garrulous spider monkey postured on the knap of her bare right shoulder. She drew heavily on the ivory cigarette holder, offered a brief, inly smile to her hosts and exhaled into the ruddled faces of Dick and Trudi.

'And you really believe,' Dick said in earnest, his tall frame as unkinked as his questioning, 'that your best work is produced in, what can I say, *puris naturalibus?*'

'*Natürlich*, naturally.' Nebulous filming obscured heavy breasts composed simply of large, concentric circles. 'An artist must have total freedom from the indoctrinations of society. We must free our body from the shackles of such behavioural codes in order to free our minds *nicht wahr*?'

'You sound very much like Salvador Dali.'

'*Achh Ja*, he too understood the logic of my theories.'

'*Your* theories?'

'*Ja*, he called them the *paranoiac-critical method* whereby the artist employs madness to intensify his vision.'

'I see,' Trudi clearly didn't, 'yet instead of melting watches you've chosen a rather unusual, er, for want of a better word, *muse*.'

The camera focused on a series of canvases interpretations of which were clouded by Hilda's dementia-shaped world.

'Your exhibition has been a huge financial success,' Dick gushed, struggling to keep his eyes on her face, 'news transcended only, in the world of art, by the recent discovery of a lost Goya painting.'

'Yes,' Trudi contributed, 'it was found in a Spanish church. Of course we're particularly excited about it as we recently interviewed an artist who claimed to be the reincarnation of Goya. He spoke of a lost painting of the Duchess of Alba with their love child. I admit to having been sceptical at the time but it seems that life can sometimes be stranger than fiction. His name was John Smith'.

Anja exhaled more tobacco choking the studio air. '*Na, Ja,* I heard the interview on the television, I remember his words well. "A great name for Sunday or ceremonial use," he said. Very amusing. *Sehr schön.* He is of course a good friend of mine.'

'Really? We didn't know that. Then as a friend do you believe that he really is the reincarnation of Goya?'

'Of course of course, the matter is under disputed.'

'You mean undisputed?'

'*Achh Ja* votever.'

✳

Peals of laughter reverberate across the miles. John Smith is happier to spectate, yet acknowledges his debt to the small screen. Beside him Maria, whose noble lineage would not be discovered for another two years, reclines easily into his zealous form. He still marvels at the sight of her yet longs for a time when it becomes more commonplace, when her expressions can pass by him like cirrus clouds, without the need for analysis. Perhaps he has become old because in her he has lost all wanderlust, like a disenchanted wayfarer who at last, having discovered his idyll, relinquishes vagrancy. He knows if she leaves him again he would be lost. His arm falls loosely about her shoulder as though to make provision for any sudden attempt at departure. He acknowledges his fear whenever she exits the room but is no longer consumed by it. He relaxes more each day into the life he has recovered. Her memories stir like a restless cobra. He nestles into the crook of each tender remembrance, urgently seeking diversion from those that render her remote and taciturn. But she has remembered the worst of him now and she remains.

The small girl is happy. She is put to bed in the lengthening shadows of evening. The cat with the China eyes watches as the rituals of bedtime are enacted. It is quiet now with the last streaks of red in a darkening sky, no sound as the child sleeps, just the incoherent flickering of light from the tall window. Beyond in the hush of the Cornish graveyard the ghost of Franco de Casiogy is saying his prayers. Or perhaps it is the sounds of the gargoyles on the church roof, their gullets filled with the spirits of the ages, or else the astral goblins plotting some future mischief? Whatever it is the world is addressed with a new civility. Wild flowers, the best variety that no one can name, are in prime bloom and there will be more to follow.

*

About the Author

Jacqueline Puchtler was born in Northamptonshire. She travelled alone to California in her late teens where she wrote articles and short stories for the High Desert Life magazine. While there she developed a fascination for Native American culture and shamanism. She married a German instructor pilot and had two sons, later living in Germany where she taught English and aerobics for a *Volkshochschule*. She has a first-class degree in Art History and Art. She now lives in England and works as a librarian for a large state school in Buckinghamshire. She paints and writes, enjoying in particular the disruption that magical realism can bring to a narrative.